Roaring Fork
ROUGHSTOCK

USA TODAY BESTSELLING AUTHOR

HEATHER SLADE

ROARING FORK ROUGHSTOCK

© 2025 Heather Slade

All rights reserved. No part of this book may be used or reproduced in any manner whatsoever without written permission, except in the case of brief quotations embodied in critical articles and reviews.
This book is a work of fiction. The names, characters, places and incidents are products of the writer's imagination or have been used fictitiously and are not to be construed as real. Any resemblance to persons, living or dead, actual events, locale or organizations is entirely coincidental.

979-8-88649-314-6

A complete list of Heather Slade's
series and titles is available at
the end of this book or,
visit her website:
HEATHERSLADE.COM

Table of Contents

1

I gripped the steering wheel of my truck until my knuckles whitened, staring at the weathered sign marking the entrance to Morris Ranch. Snow drifted lazily in my headlights—another February storm settling over Parlin like a shroud. Fitting, given I felt like I was driving to my own funeral.

The envelope from the attorney lay crumpled on the passenger seat, its contents burned in my mind: Go to Morris Ranch. Stay one year. Save it, or lose everything. The words of our family attorney, Six-Pack, who'd read the codicil, echoed in my head—three hundred and sixty-five days, no absences longer than forty-eight consecutive hours, or my siblings and I lose everything. Including the Roaring Fork. My family's legacy. All because of one vindictive asshole—my father—whose plot for revenge changed what might've been a happy family. Maybe if the *sonuvabitch* had faced an early death rather than my mother, we could've been.

But it wasn't him dictating where and how I'd spend the next year of my life. No, it was a nameless, faceless trustee who hid behind a ghost trust filed in New Mexico, one of the few remaining states that allowed the legal document to be written in such a way that the trustee's identity remained protected.

He or she controlled my fate and that of my siblings. I was the third who'd had to adhere to another of the trust's codicils or we'd lose everything. The ranch, the roughstock business I'd built, which was finally turning a profit, but more importantly, our heritage. I couldn't be the one who allowed that to happen.

The irony wasn't lost on me that I was once again sacrificing myself, keeping secrets to protect others. How long had I held on to the truth about my oldest brother, Buck? Since I was eight years old, when my drunk father, Roscoe, had used it to justify his cruelty. Secrets had a way of snowballing in my family, each one gathering weight until they threatened to bury us all.

That wasn't the only secret pressing against my conscience. The second was the truth of what had happened the night Maverick Morris came close to losing his life.

Somehow, that nameless, faceless fucker of a trustee who was determining our collective destiny found out about the accident. The one that had nearly destroyed a family. Not mine but the Morris'. What was left of them.

I scrubbed my face with my hand as Maverick's words echoed in my head for the thousandth time. "Promise me you won't tell my sister. It'll destroy her." The kid had been barely conscious—so much so he didn't recall anything from that night. Blood had been streaming from a gash in his forehead, his leg bent at an impossible angle. I'd given him my vow that night, knowing it could cost me everything. But what it would've cost him was far greater. The kid was only seventeen.

Now, here I was, about to face her—the woman who'd once said she loved me, but now hated me with every fiber of her being. Not that I blamed her. As far as Cici knew, I was the drunk driver who had nearly killed her only remaining family.

The ranch house loomed ahead, a single light burning in an upstairs window despite the early hour. I cut my engine, listening to it tick in the predawn silence. The forecast called for eight inches of snow, and I needed to get the lay of the land before the storm hit in earnest.

I grabbed my duffel from the backseat and forced myself to walk toward the house, my boots crunching on the frozen gravel. Better to face Cici now and get the inevitable confrontation over with.

Movement caught my eye—a figure in the barn's doorway. Even in the dim light, I recognized Cici's stance and the defiant tilt of her chin. She had a rifle propped against her shoulder.

"That's far enough, Wheaton."

Her voice carried clearly in the still air, cold as the snow swirling between us. I stopped, raising my hands slightly.

"I'm not here to cause trouble, Cici."

"I'm Cicily to you. Better yet, Ms. Morris. Only my friends call me Cici, and you sure as fuck aren't one of them." She took a step forward, rifle unwavering. "Now, get off my land!"

I kept my voice level, unthreatening. "I'm here to help."

Her bitter laugh cut through me. "Help? Like you helped my brother? Get back in your damn truck and leave. I'd rather watch this place burn than accept anything from you."

I held my ground, arms in the air. "I can't do that."

"Can't?" She cackled. "What happened? Your own family tossed you out on your ear?"

I lowered my hands slowly. "I have my reasons for being here, Cicily. Whether you believe it or not, saving this ranch matters to me."

"The only thing that matters to you is the bottom of a whiskey bottle." Her words were meant to wound, and they hit their mark. "You're not welcome here."

"I understand that. But I'm not leaving." I took a careful step forward. "You need someone who knows roughstock contracting. Your operation is bleeding money."

"And whose fault is that?" The rifle barrel tracked my movement. "We lost half our contracts after your outfit undercut us. Somehow, you found out our bid and lowered yours. You're a stupid asshole if you think I don't know it. Not to mention, you're a dirty drunk."

"I'm sober now." It was true—it had been close to two months since I last had a drink. "And I know how to rebuild your stock program."

"It was fine before *you* contributed to its demise." She finally lowered the rifle, but her stance remained rigid with hostility. "You have five minutes to get off my property before I call Kaleb."

Kaleb Ackerman was the sheriff of Gunnison County and the only man who knew the secret I kept about Cici's brother.

I reached into my jacket and slowly withdrew the folded papers I shouldn't have in my possession, but did. "You'll want to read this first."

"I'm not reading anything from you."

"It's not from me. It's from your bank." I held the documents out. "Your last loan extension expires in thirty days. After that, they'll start foreclosure proceedings."

Cici stared at the papers like they might bite her. Finally, she snatched them from my hand, scanning them quickly in the growing light. Her face paled.

"This is private financial information. How did you get this?"

"Does it matter? What matters is I can help you prevent it from happening." I gestured to the barn behind her. "Let me prove it to you. One month. If you're not seeing improvement by then, I'll leave."

She studied me for a long moment, jaw clenched. The snow was falling harder now, collecting on her dark hair.

"You're seriously going to lose your family's ranch because it's me offering help? Come on, Cici. We both know you're smarter than that."

She bristled at my words, then hung her head. "One month," she finally bit out. "But if you come anywhere near my brother, if you so much as look at him wrong, I'll kill you. Are we clear?"

I nodded once. "Crystal clear."

She turned on her heel and stalked toward the barn. "The north bunkhouse is that way. Stay out of the main house. And, Wheaton?"

I paused, waiting.

"Don't mistake this for forgiveness. I'll never forgive you for what you did to Maverick."

I watched her disappear into the barn, shoulders straight and proud despite the weight of worry I knew she felt on them. My own were weighted too, with both the secret I carried for her brother and the real reason I'd shown up here this morning.

I had one month to prove myself. Then one year to save the ranch and somehow keep my promise to

Maverick while facing the sister who had every reason to despise me.

I shouldered my bag and headed for the bunkhouse. The storm was rolling in, and I had work to do.

The place designated for the ranch hands to sleep was barely more than a shack, with gaps in the wooden walls, where the wind whistled through. Inside, a thin layer of dust covered everything—the narrow cots, the rickety table, the pot-bellied stove in the corner. No one had lived here for a while. That told me more about the ranch's financial situation than any bank documents could.

I tossed my duffel on the table and dug out my flashlight. The beam revealed cobwebs in the corners and mouse droppings along the baseboards. Perfect. I'd slept in worse places during my roughneck days, but this was going to need work before the serious storm hit.

My phone buzzed—another message from Cord. I'd been ignoring my family's calls since leaving the attorney's office. What could I say? Sorry, I lied again? Sorry, the secrets I carry aren't my own? Sorry, I can't tell you the hell most of my life has been and why?

A month ago, I'd almost lost the brother I was closer to than any of my other siblings. A couple of weeks before Christmas, Cord got word from our family's attorney that, according to a codicil in the Roaring Fork Trust similar to the one that required me to come here to Morris Ranch, he had to report to a town in New York, not far from Buffalo. He was instructed to show up at an estate called the Lilacs, live there for a year, and step into the role of livestock manager. At the time, none of us understood why he had to leave Colorado, where he'd spent his whole life, to go live in a place he'd never heard of.

We still didn't know exactly why, but a month after he got there—which just so happened to be the night after my accident with Mav—while checking on cattle during a snowstorm, he was attacked and left for dead.

That he was still alive was a fucking miracle. A team of EMTs and doctors literally brought him back from the dead, and over the course of the last five weeks, he'd come out of a coma and learned to talk and walk again. Buck, Holt, and our sister, Flynn, took turns flying to New York and spending time at the hospital with him. Given I was in jail when it happened and still not cleared to leave the State of Colorado, I was the only one unable to be there for him. It still ate at me, no matter how many times Cord said he'd forgiven me. And, like everyone else, he still believed I drove drunk that night and almost killed Cici's younger brother.

I'd swear Cord had somehow sensed there was more to what happened that night, but he hadn't pushed, and I was grateful for that.

His message was brief. *Be careful,* it read. If he only knew the thing I needed to protect more than our ranch was Cici's heart. I'd broken it twice now. I couldn't do it again.

I started a fire in the stove with the meager supply of wood stacked beside it. The flames cast dancing shadows on the walls as I did a proper inspection of my temporary home. The roof seemed solid enough, but the windows needed weatherstripping. The bathroom was functional, barely. At least there was running water.

Outside, the storm was picking up intensity. Through the grimy window, I could see lights on in the barn where Cici had disappeared. The smart thing would be to stay put, let her cool down. But I needed to see the condition of the stock before this weather got worse.

I pulled on my heavy winter duster and grabbed my work gloves. The wind nearly yanked the bunkhouse door from my hands as I stepped out. Already, the snow was a good two inches deep. The barn wasn't far—maybe fifty yards—but in this weather, it might as well have been a mile.

I made it halfway there before I heard the screaming of a horse in pain.

My heart lurched. Without thinking, I broke into a run. That sound meant trouble—big trouble. I hit the barn door at full speed, shouldering it open.

The scene inside stopped me cold. Cici was struggling with a massive stallion who'd gotten his leg tangled in a lead rope. The horse's eyes were wild with panic, his nostrils flaring.

"Stay back!" Cici shouted when she saw me. But the horse chose that moment to rear, jerking her off her feet.

I didn't hesitate. I dove forward, tackling her out of the way as the stallion's hooves crashed down where she'd fallen. We hit the hay-covered floor hard, my body blanketing hers.

"I told you to stay back," she snarled, shoving at my chest.

"You're welcome," I muttered, rolling to my feet and tugging off my coat. The stallion was still thrashing, the rope cutting deeper into his leg. "That's Thunder Cloud, isn't it?"

Her eyes narrowed. "How do you know that?"

"Because I was the one who helped your dad pick him out." I kept my voice steady, soothing, as I approached the horse. "Easy, boy. Remember me?"

The stallion's ears flicked forward. His breathing was still rapid, but some of the panic left his eyes. I kept talking softly as I edged closer, letting him catch my scent.

"I didn't know you were there." Cici's voice was barely a whisper.

"Sure was. Your father knew horses better than anyone I've ever met." I was close enough now to touch Thunder Cloud's neck. "He taught me a lot about what to look for when bidding on horses. Bulls too."

The stallion relaxed slightly under my touch. I used the moment to assess the situation with the rope. It was wrapped tightly, but hadn't cut off circulation yet. With careful maneuvering, I could get it free.

"I need your help," I said without looking at Cici. "Can you set aside hating me long enough to keep this horse from losing his leg?"

There was a long pause. Then she moved to Thunder Cloud's head, stroking his nose. "What do you need me to do?"

We worked in tense silence for several minutes. Her hands were steady as she kept the stallion calm while I gently unwound the rope. When the last loop came free, we both breathed a sigh of relief.

Thunder Cloud shook himself, then nudged Cici's shoulder as if nothing had happened. She pressed her forehead to his neck for a moment.

"Thank you," she finally said, not looking at me. "But don't think this changes anything."

"I know." I coiled the offending lead rope, using the task to hide whatever emotion might show on my face. "But you should know—I meant what I said about helping. Your dad was a good man. He taught me a lot, and when I heard about the accident…I'm sorry I wasn't here for you and Mav, Cici."

"Don't." Her voice cracked. "Don't talk about my father. Don't talk about my brother. Just…don't."

She was gone before I could respond, the barn's side door slamming behind her. Thunder Cloud watched her go, then turned his knowing eyes in my direction, as though he was judging me.

"Yeah, I know, boy," I said, patting his neck. "I've got my work cut out for me."

The storm howled outside, but I stayed in the barn for a long time, checking every stall and every piece of equipment. The place was falling apart. No matter where I looked, I saw something that needed to be repaired or replaced. But under the worn exterior, the bones were good. Like the ranch itself.

I had to figure out how to save it without destroying what little trust Cici had left in the world. And somehow keep the promise that was eating me alive.

Thunder Cloud nickered softly as I headed for the door. I paused, looking back at him. "Keep your leg out of trouble next time, okay? She might not let me stick around long enough to help again."

I prayed I was wrong. I needed to be here for the long haul, whether Cici wanted me to be or not. I had no choice.

The wind bit into me as I made my way back to the bunkhouse. Tomorrow, the real struggle would begin. Today, we just had to survive the storm—both the one outside, and the one brewing in my heart every time I looked at Cici Morris.

2

Cici

I slammed the farmhouse door behind me, my hands shaking as I peeled off my snow-crusted coat. Damn Porter Wheaton. Damn him for showing up here. Damn him for saving Thunder Cloud. And damn him most of all for reminding me of how things used to be.

The kitchen was dark and cold. I hadn't bothered relighting the wood stove when I saw his truck approaching. Now, I crouched in front of it, willing my fingers to stop trembling long enough to get a fire started.

"Cici?" Maverick's voice came from the doorway. "I heard voices outside. Was—" He stopped when he saw my face, squared his shoulders, and continued. "Was that Porter Wheaton I saw headed into the bunkhouse?"

I nodded, not trusting my voice. The kindling finally caught, and I added larger pieces of wood, anything to avoid looking at my brother.

"What's he doing here?"

I rolled my shoulders, wishing I had more time to come up with a story to cover what was really happening to our ranch.

"I'll go talk to him." 1:07 pronunciation Mav's crutches clicked against the wooden floor as he moved farther into the kitchen. He didn't need them all the time. Mainly when he was worn out, which had been happening more frequently lately.

"No." The word came out sharper than I'd intended. I stood, facing him. "You're not going anywhere near him."

Maverick's face darkened. At seventeen, he was trying so hard to be a man, to carry his share of the burden. But I saw the pain in his eyes every time he looked at his mangled leg and saw his dreams of bull-riding championships dying a little more each day.

"I can handle myself," he muttered.

"I know you can." I softened my tone. "But Porter Wheaton is not coming within fifty feet of you. Not after what he did."

Something flickered across Mav's face—guilt maybe, or fear. But it was gone so quickly I might have imagined it.

"Why is he here?" he asked a second time.

I sighed, wishing I could shield my brother from this news, but Porter being here made that impossible.

"He brought this." I pulled the crumpled bank papers from my pocket, scanning them again. "He says he can help." I laughed bitterly. "As if he hasn't done enough 'helping' already."

Mav took the document and studied it.

"This is bad, Cici."

"I know, and I'm sorry."

"Did you really think I didn't know?" he accused as much as asked.

"What do you mean?"

He sneered, an expression I saw too often lately. "I knew how much trouble the ranch was in. Is in."

"We're managing."

"Are we? Because these papers say differently."

I sighed, sinking into one of the kitchen chairs. "It's just temporary cash flow issues. Once spring comes—"

"*Spring?* This says we have thirty days, Cici. We don't have time to fuck around—"

"Watch your language," I snapped.

"Sorry," he mumbled, looking down at the floor, then maneuvering himself into the chair across from me. "All I'm saying is why not let him help us? Porter knows this business. He has connections—"

"Connections?" I stood so abruptly that my chair scraped against the floor. "The only connection that matters is the one between his drunk driving and your destroyed leg. Or did you forget that part?"

Mav flinched. "I haven't forgotten anything, but it seems you have."

"What does that mean?"

"I'm seventeen, not seven. You treat me like a damn kid."

"I'm sorry—"

"Don't be. Just quit lying to me all the time." His tone made me pause, and his words hung heavy in the air, weighted with something I couldn't allow myself to think about. The way his voice sometimes caught. The way he so often refused to meet my eyes. I wasn't surprised when he turned around and left the room, angry like he always seemed to be.

I stood and looked out the window at the worsening storm. The wind from it rattled the windows. We needed new ones; there just wasn't any money to pay for things that, now, felt more like a luxury than a necessity. I went into the kitchen, stunned to see Mav standing there.

"I need to check on the horses," I said, reaching for my coat.

"Cici—"

"Get some rest, Mav. I'll bring up some soup when I'm done."

"You can't keep avoiding this conversation forever," he called after me. "About Porter, about the ranch, about Mom and Dad."

I froze with my hand on the doorknob. "What about Mom and Dad?"

"Don't you ever wonder why they were out on that road that night? The timing never made sense, Cici. Dad knew better than to drive in weather like that, especially with Mom—"

"Stop." My voice cracked. "Just stop. They hit a patch of black ice. It was an accident. End of story."

Mav met my gaze steadily. "Because I'm not blind, sis. And neither were they. Something was going on at the ranch before they died. Something bad enough that Dad was worried we might lose it, the same way—"

"That's not true," I snapped. But even as I said it, memories surfaced—hushed conversations behind closed doors, Dad's worried frown as he reviewed the books late at night, Mom's insistence that we learn to shoot, to defend ourselves. "They would have told us."

"Would they? Like you tell me everything?" His eyes were too knowing. "Like you told me about the rest of the letters? And I don't mean from the bank. I mean the threatening ones."

My breath caught. I'd found the first two weeks ago, shoved under the front door. Crude letters cut from magazines spelling out, "SELL OR SUFFER." I'd burned it before Mav could see it. It hadn't been the last of them, though.

I escaped into the storm before he could say more. The truth was, I couldn't bear to see the defeat in his eyes. Not when I was supposed to be the strong one—the older sister. Not when I was failing so miserably at keeping our family legacy alive.

And not when he was getting too close to the questions I wasn't ready to answer. Questions about our parents' death, about the ranch's sudden decline, about why Porter Wheaton's arrival felt less like coincidence and more like another piece of a puzzle I couldn't quite fit together.

Snow stung my face as I made my way back to the barn. Through the swirling white, I could see Porter's figure moving between the outbuildings, no doubt taking stock of everything we'd let fall into disrepair. Everything I'd failed to maintain since Dad died.

The sight of him made my chest ache with a confusion of emotions—anger, yes, but also a traitorous flutter of something else. Feelings from the past that I'd buried long ago. Just not deep enough.

The way he'd moved so quickly to save me from Thunder Cloud, the gentleness in his hands as he'd freed the stallion's leg, the raw honesty in his voice when he'd spoken about my dad—it all brought back memories that threatened to rip me to shreds.

Those thoughts were too dangerous. Porter Wheaton had wrecked me in ways that had nothing to do with drunk driving and everything to do with how easy it had been for me to accept his help. Why had I? Was I really that weak? God, I made myself sick.

I gritted my teeth and pushed forward. It wasn't like I had a choice. No one else had shown up, offering their help. I had one month to turn things around. Surely, I could endure his presence that long. And then, he'd be gone, taking his guilt and his memories and his damn hero complex with him.

But Mav's words echoed in my head. Something had been going on at the ranch before our parents died. Something that might explain the letters, the financial troubles, and the whispered rumors in town about a curse on Morris land. That was the one that hit me the hardest. There were times it sure was easy to think our family was cursed.

As I reached the barn door, Thunder Cloud's wild eyes flashed in my memory. If Porter hadn't been there…

No. I wouldn't go down that road. I couldn't afford gratitude, couldn't afford to see him as anything but the man who'd destroyed my brother's future. The man who'd shown up uninvited to witness our slow decline, holding a letter from the bank he had no business getting his hands on.

One month. That was all. I just had to keep my walls up that long.

"You okay?" Porter's voice carried through the snow, closer than I'd realized. He stood a few yards away, watching me with those damn perceptive eyes. "You've been standing there…"

"I'm fine." The words came automatically, the same lie I'd been telling for months. Years, maybe.

He nodded slowly. "Sure you are, Cici."

Before I could tell him to fuck off, he turned away, disappearing into the white curtain of snow like a ghost.

I just had to keep reminding myself that Porter Wheaton was the enemy. No matter what my treacherous heart felt when he'd tackled me out of harm's way. No matter how his voice had softened when he spoke about my dad. No matter how the bad news kept piling up, threatening to bury me like the endless February snow.

One month, then everything could go back to normal.

If only I could convince myself that "normal" wasn't just another word for watching everything I loved slip away, one piece at a time.

3

Porter

The sun was just rising the following morning when I headed out to assess the damage from yesterday's storm. My muscles ached from sleeping on the bunkhouse cot, but it was nothing compared to the weight in my chest every time I thought about Cici's face when I'd mentioned her father. I supposed I had a similar expression when someone talked about my mother, but even then, it wasn't with the same love and admiration she conveyed.

On approach, it appeared the main barn had weathered the storm nicely enough, but the smaller outbuildings hadn't fared as well. Shingles littered the ground, and one of the storage sheds was tilting dangerously to one side. I made mental notes as I walked the property, cataloging everything that needed to be repaired. The list kept growing, and not all the damage was weather related. It was clear that much of it had gradually happened in the time since no one was here to fix it. Cici was capable, of course, but some things needed money. A lot of it. And it was abundantly clear that was in short supply.

A light flickered on in the ranch house's kitchen, and through the window, I caught a glimpse of her moving around, probably starting coffee. Part of me wanted to offer to help with the morning chores, but after last night's confrontation over Thunder Cloud, I knew better.

Instead, I headed for the roughstock pens. This was where Morris Ranch's real problems would present themselves. Sure enough, the first thing I noticed was the poor condition of the fencing. No self-respecting rodeo would contract with an outfit that couldn't properly contain their animals.

Later, once I'd completed an initial plan of attack, I'd call Buck to see which hands the Roaring Fork could spare for a few days. If I had my pick, I'd ask for three, all of whom hailed from Gunnison County.

First, Bullet Simmons, an NFR bull-riding champion who came to work for us once he decided he'd had enough of climbing on the back of one-ton animals to prove he could stay on for eight seconds. Second, Stetson Hamilton, also an NFR champ, but on bucking broncs. His father had developed the equine breeding program we used on our ranch. Lastly, Nash "Thorn" Roseman, who was the assistant ranch foreman. That decision would be up to Bridger West, who took over managing the roughstock operation when Cord and I were forced to leave because some asshole had decided to fuck with our inheritance.

"That bad?" I turned to find Cici standing behind me, arms crossed against the cold. Her dark hair was pulled back in a severe braid, but a few strands had escaped to frame her face. Even angry, she was beautiful.

"Pardon?"

"By the look of disgust on your face, I assume you're looking for more things to criticize."

Since I couldn't explain that what I was really disgusted with was a nameless, faceless control freak fucking with the lives of my siblings and me, I gestured to the nearest section of fence. "These posts won't last another month."

"You think I don't know that?" Her voice was sharp. "You think I haven't tried—" She stopped, pressing her lips together.

"Tried what?"

"Nothing. Just stay out of my way." She started to turn away.

"It's too late for Fort Worth and San Antonio, but the RodeoHouston is a possibility, especially if someone drops out," I said. "You planning to submit a bid?"

That stopped her. "I already did, but after the accident..." She shrugged, trying to look like it didn't matter. "They don't want us there."

"Wrong. They don't want an outfit that won't deliver as promised," I corrected. "But I've already talked to the board. They'll reconsider if you let me handle the stock."

She spun around. "You *what*?"

"I sent some messages last night. They know me, trust me. Or they did. Anyway..." I scrubbed my face. "Look, this could be your chance to rebuild your reputation. Our reputation."

"Our reputation?" She laughed bitterly. "There is no 'our' anything, Wheaton. And I don't need your help with the board."

"Really? Because last I heard, you were down to three major contracts for the year. That won't cover your operating costs, let alone the bank loan."

Her eyes narrowed. "You seem to know an awful lot about my business."

More than you realize, I thought. But I couldn't tell her I'd spent the last six months tracking Morris Ranch's decline, watching helplessly as everything Hank Morris had built crumbled after his death. Then, I told myself it had been out of concern for another roughstocker in the area, not because my heart beat harder every time Cici crossed my mind. Which was far too often. I'd wake at night, remembering how her naked body had felt under mine. How there was no greater pleasure in the world than burying myself deep in her heat.

"RodeoHouston could change everything. The total purse is over two million dollars," I said, hoping she hadn't noticed the redness that crept up my neck, thinking about her that way. "But you need better stock than what I'm seeing here. Half these broncs look past their prime."

"They're experienced."

"They're tired. And your bulls…" I gestured to the pen, where three massive animals huddled against the cold. "When was the last time you ran a genetic testing? Because that red one has the same markings as—"

"Who the fuck do you think you are, coming in here telling me how to run my own program?"

I sighed. "He has the same markings as his grandfather, Cici. You're breeding too close to the bloodline. It'll affect their performance. Maybe it already has."

Color rose in her cheeks. "So now, you're an expert on that too?"

"I'm sure your father taught you about—"

She held up a hand. "I told you not to talk about him."

"Fine." I pulled a folded paper from my pocket. "But at least look at this. It's a preliminary contract for the Houston. All it needs is your signature."

She stared at the paper like it might bite her. "You filled this out last night?"

"Consider it a peace offering," I said, hoping she wouldn't pick up on me not answering her question.

"I don't want peace with you."

"Then, consider it business. The ranch needs this. *You* need it."

For a moment, I thought she might actually take the contract. But then, she stepped back, shaking her head.

"I'm late for feeding." She started toward the barn, then paused. "Fix the fence if you want. But stay away from the bull-stud program. That was my father's pride and joy, and I won't let you ruin that too."

I watched her go, the contract still clutched in my hand. Hank Morris had been more than proud of what he developed—he'd been innovative and forward-thinking. He would've seen the problems I saw and would've already been working to fix them. My guess was Cici had been forced to sell her best stock, figuring what was left would be good enough. If I was right, it was the worst thing she could've done. Instead, she should've focused on breeding fees, including negotiating that some of the stock born would go to Morris Ranch.

When I set out to develop the program at the Roaring Fork, I talked to as many of the contractors in the area I could, including her father.

But I couldn't tell Cici that. I couldn't tell her the real reason I'd approached him in the first place. How I'd hoped to get one glimpse of her. To know she was okay. Or about the many hours I'd spent with him, learning everything he knew about roughstock. And I couldn't tell her that the last time I saw him alive, he'd asked me to look out for his kids if anything ever happened to him.

It was as though he'd had a premonition, and I'd failed him spectacularly.

A sound from the ranch house caught my attention. Maverick stood at his bedroom window, watching me. When our eyes met, he quickly disappeared behind the curtain.

The kid was carrying as many secrets as I was. And if we both weren't careful, they'd eventually come crashing down around us.

I shoved the contract back in my pocket and headed for the tool shed. The fence wouldn't fix itself, and right now, it was the only thing I could control.

At the top of the list of things I couldn't was how in the hell, at the end of the first month, I'd be able to convince Cici that I needed to stay eleven more. If I didn't, my brothers, sister, and I would lose everything. Telling her that wouldn't earn me any sympathy, though. She was already of the mind that everything I touched turned to ruin. I doubted she'd listen long enough to clarify or even care that what my family faced wasn't my doing. The only thing that was, was my reason for landing here, and that, I could never tell her.

After a long, hard day, ticking off the list of things that needed to be fixed without taking as much as a break to eat, I fell on the cot, hoping exhaustion alone would help me sleep.

Instead, after placing the call to Buck I'd intended to earlier, I lay on the lumpy pad that was supposed to substitute for a mattress and stared at the ceiling. I'd ask God, a higher power, or the universe how the fuck I ended up here, but that answer was abundantly clear. I'd lived a shit life and got what I deserved.

After a couple of hours, my muscles already ached and harrowing thoughts continued swirling in my head.

Morris Ranch's rapid decline weighed heavily on me as I got up, turned on a light, and pored over the records I'd already read enough to have memorized. Numbers swam before my eyes—genetic markers, performance ratings, bloodline charts. I recognized Hank Morris's innovative touches being slowly eroded by necessity and mismanagement. Each page reminded me of time spent in his office, learning his methods. It was invaluable knowledge I hoped I could share with Cici one day. Tell her how many times I was here when she wasn't. Hank had been careful about that. God, I wanted to talk to her about the fond memories I had of a man who'd treated me far better than my own father ever had.

I was still awake well after midnight, rereading the same things again and again and knowing disaster loomed if someone didn't intervene soon. The only saving grace, as I saw it, was that Buck had agreed to send over the three men I asked for and, more importantly, keep them on the Roaring Fork payroll for however long they were here. They'd arrive first thing tomorrow morning and would bring some of our other hands, all of whom would be prepared to get right to work.

I stood, thinking about attempting to get some rest, when a flicker of movement caught my eye through the window—an orange glow reflecting off the northwest barn's metal roof.

I jumped up, stuck my feet in my boots, grabbed my coat, and raced from the bunkhouse. The acrid smell of accelerant hit me before I'd fully processed what I was seeing. This was no accident. The flame pattern was too deliberate and spreading too fast.

I slammed my hand on the emergency alarm on one of the closer outbuildings, pulled my cell from my coat pocket, and called one of the ranch's few remaining hands, who was likely fast asleep in the other bunkhouse. My voice cracked when the man answered. "Johnson, fire in the northwest barn! We need everybody! Wake up Martinez and Shaw, and get the trailers to the back alley doors. *Now!*"

The night air bit through my shirt as I sprinted across the yard. Heat blasted my face when I wrenched the front door open. Inside, the animals had worked themselves into a frenzy. Smoke curled along the ceiling beams, and flames licked up the far wall. The horses screamed—high, terrified sounds that made my skin crawl.

Past experience from fires at the Roaring Fork, along with Hank's training, kicked in. I moved methodically despite the chaos, things I'd learned echoing in my head. "A scared horse is a dangerous horse. You gotta be their calm," Cici's father said in my head. I started with the nearest stalls, leading them out in pairs, one hand on each lead rope. The frightened animals fought me at first, but I kept my movements unhurried, my voice low. "Easy now. That's it."

Embers rained down, burning holes in my coat and searing my exposed skin. I ignored the pain. Six horses out. Eight. Ten. The smoke grew thicker as sirens sounded in the distance, still too far away, in my estimation. What the fuck was taking them so long to get here?

Then I heard it—a familiar whinny through the roar of flames. *Thunder Cloud.* The stallion was trapped in the back corner, a fallen support beam blocking his stall. The horse's bloodline alone was worth more than most of the ranch's contracts, but it wasn't just about money. This was Hank's pride and joy, the cornerstone of his equine program.

I wrapped my bandanna around my face and crawled under the worst of the smoke. The beam was heavy, but fear and adrenaline gave me the necessary strength. My shoulders screamed as I heaved it aside. Thunder Cloud's eyes rolled white with terror, but he knew me. When I reached for his halter, he didn't fight.

We burst out of the barn together just as Cici pulled up and leaped from the cab of her truck. The light from the fire painted her ghost-white face as she ran over.

Our eyes met, and in them, I saw relief warring with suspicion. Before I could say a word, fire trucks pulled in. They weren't just from Parlin; units from Gunnison, Crested Butte, and Montrose arrived minutes later, but by then, her crew and I had saved what mattered most.

I wanted to tell her my suspicions, that the fire had been set deliberately, but there was no time for that now. Instead, I joined the hands Johnson had roused, along with those from nearby ranches he must've called for support. I focused on treating the horses and cattle for smoke inhalation, checking each one for burns while trying to ignore the stinging of my own.

When Kaleb arrived to take statements from us and the fire chief, I couldn't help but notice the looks Cici shot me while we answered the sheriff's questions. That her expression of gratitude was mixed with distrust burned worse than my injuries.

When she approached Thunder Cloud, running her hands over him, I saw tears in her eyes she quickly blinked away.

"Thank you," she whispered so quietly I almost missed it. "You should get those burns looked at." I nodded, watching her lead her father's prized stallion to safety to the smaller pasture that was closest to the house.

"I smell gasoline," Kaleb said in a low tone of voice when he came to stand beside me. "The chief is calling in an arson investigator."

The ranch's problems went deeper than bad fencing and poor breeding choices. Someone wanted Morris Ranch to fail, and they were willing to burn it to the ground to make that happen.

4

Cici

The smell of smoke still clung to my clothes, so I went upstairs to change before returning to my dad's office. I stared at the financial reports that had been spread out on his desk for days. The leather of his chair creaked as I leaned back, trying to sort through the mess of emotions churning inside me. Outside, the sun was barely cresting the horizon, painting the snow-covered yard in shades of pink.

Sometimes, I swore I could hear him here, late at night, muttering over contracts or calling his old rodeo buddies to arrange deals. He'd built this place from nothing, turned a rundown cattle ranch into a well-respected roughstock operation. And in my less-than-capable hands, it was crumbling.

I shook, picking up the latest reports I'd generated from the ranch's antiquated accounting software. The numbers reinforced what I'd known for months—we were hemorrhaging money faster than I could patch the holes. And now, with the fire damage…I dropped the paper and pressed my palms against my eyes, fighting back tears of exhaustion and frustration.

The image of Porter rushing into flames to save our stock kept replaying in my mind. The way he'd known exactly which horses and bulls to prioritize, as if he understood their value beyond dollars and cents. It was the kind of knowledge that came from experience—the kind Dad would have appreciated.

A sound at the door made me jump. I looked up at Porter, who stood in the doorway. His face was streaked with soot, and burns were visible on his forearms where his sleeves had rolled up. The sight of him in my father's sanctuary sent an irrational surge of anger through me.

"I, err, knocked," he said. "The sheriff needs your signature on some forms," he added in a voice rough from smoke inhalation when I nodded. He didn't step into the room, instead maintaining the careful distance I'd demanded. Smart man.

I nodded again, not trusting myself to speak. The memory of him emerging from the flames with Thunder Cloud was still too fresh, too confusing. It didn't fit with the image I'd built of him over the past couple of years—especially over the last one when all I could see was the reckless drunk who'd nearly killed my brother. The man who'd almost destroyed what little there was left of my life with one night of the worst kind of stupidity.

"The fire chief suspects arson," he continued when I didn't respond. "They found accelerant patterns. Whoever did this knew what they were doing."

"Who would…?" I stopped, remembering not only the recently received threatening letters but the whispered conversations I'd overheard between my parents before the accident.

Then, it was about the mounting pressure from the developers eyeing our land that I believed fueled my dad's paranoia in those final weeks.

"Someone who wants the ranch to fail." He pulled a folded paper from his pocket—the Houston contract he'd tried to give me yesterday. "This could help stop that from happening. But only if you'll agree to it."

Pride warred with pragmatism as I stared at the papers. Every instinct screamed at me not to trust him, but the numbers didn't lie. Without major contracts, we'd lose everything within months. Mom and Dad's legacy would vanish like morning frost under a harsh sun.

"Show me." The words felt like gravel in my throat.

"What?"

"Show me what's wrong with the operation. Everything." I gestured to the chair across from the desk—Dad's guest chair. My stomach twisted at the sight of Porter settling into it, but I forced the feeling down. "You've been here two days and already spotted problems I missed. So show me."

Porter hesitated only for a moment before pulling out a notebook filled with his cramped handwriting. Pages of detailed observations about our stock and our facilities. The thoroughness surprised me—he must have been up half the night documenting everything.

"Your father had a system," he began, and for once, I didn't stop him from mentioning Dad. "He tracked genetic lines, performance ratings, health records—everything that made Morris Ranch's roughstock program as respected as it was. In order to give you an accurate picture of where that stands now, we'd need to do the testing I mentioned before." He flipped through several pages. "Here's what we'd need to evaluate."

As he walked me through the list, I felt my confidence crumbling. Possible problems I hadn't allowed myself to think about were laid bare—inbreeding risks, declining performance metrics, missed health screenings. Every word was evidence of my incompetence, but I forced myself to listen.

"See these charts?" He spread out several papers. "Your father was careful about genetic diversity, but in the last year, you've had to sell off key bloodlines. The remaining stock is too closely related."

I'd heard him the first time he mentioned the markings indicative of bloodlines. That I'd been so focused on keeping the lights on was no excuse for me missing the bigger picture. Dad's meticulously crafted program was dissolving under my watch because I'd sold the wrong animals.

"The Houston contract is just the beginning," he said, his voice softening. "But we need to address these issues first, starting with—"

"We?" I cut in sharply.

He met my gaze steadily. "Yes, we. Because, like it or not, Cici, you need help. The ranch needs help. And I'm not the only one who sees it."

Through the window, I noticed Maverick making his way toward the barn, leaning heavily on the cane he used when he didn't think he needed the crutches. The sight of his halting progress hardened my resolve. This wasn't just about me. It never had been. And it wasn't about Porter. It was about preserving something bigger than all of us.

A memory surfaced—Dad standing in this very office, telling me that sometimes the hardest part of running a ranch was knowing when to swallow your pride and accept help. I'd been twelve then, watching him negotiate a loan to expand the costly programs he'd developed. Now, I understood exactly what he'd meant.

"I only agreed to one month," I finally said, the words tasting like ash in my mouth.

"You know that won't be long enough."

I scowled. Of course it wasn't. "There are conditions." I ticked them off on my fingers. "You don't speak to Maverick. You don't make major changes

without consulting me first. And you tell me everything—every problem, every solution, every detail.
No secrets."

The irony of demanding honesty from him wasn't
lost on me. Not when I had my own secrets locked
away in the desk. Not when I still couldn't explain
why our parents had been on that icy road the night
they died.

"Agreed." He didn't hesitate. "But I have a condition too." He tapped the Houston contract. "You give
this a real shot. No sabotaging it out of spite."

The accusation stung. I *had* been ready to reject the
opportunity simply because it came from him. How
many other chances would I miss if I didn't set aside
my anger?

"Fine." I snatched up a pen and signed the contract
before I could change my mind. The scratch of pen
on paper sounded final, irrevocable. "But again, don't
mistake this for forgiveness. Or trust."

"I don't." He gathered his notes and stood. In the
early morning light, the burns on his arms looked
worse—angry red welts that made me wince despite
myself. "I'll have a full assessment of the rest tonight

since now we're down a barn. I plan to include security recommendations. That fire wasn't an accident, and we both know it won't be the last attempt to destroy what's left of this place."

The certainty in his voice sent a chill down my spine. He knew something—something he wasn't telling me. But before I could press him, Maverick's voice drifted through the window, calling to one of the horses. Porter's expression shifted, something like guilt flickering across his features.

As he reached the door, I called after him. "Porter?" He paused but didn't turn. "Get those burns looked at. We can't afford to have you sidelined by infection."

He nodded once and was gone, leaving me alone with the ghost of my father and the sickening feeling that I'd just made either the best decision of my life or my worst mistake.

I turned to the window, watching him cross the yard, realizing I'd never signed the forms the sheriff needed. I went outside and walked over to him. On the way, I caught how the rising sun cast Porter's shadow long across the snow—a dark line cutting through the pristine white, like a divider between past and future. Like the one I'd just crossed by letting him back into our lives—into my life.

Dad's voice seemed to whisper from the corners of the office: "Trust your gut, little girl. But remember—sometimes the truth isn't what we think it is."

I wished I could decide which truth to focus on—the one about Porter Wheaton or the one about why he and Mom had really died that night. I couldn't shake the fear the two might be more connected than I wanted to know. Was that the real reason he was here? Did his guilt run deeper than the accident with my brother? Had he played a role in my parents' death too?

5

The numbers didn't add up.

I sat at the rickety table in the bunkhouse, surrounded by years of Morris Ranch's financial records I'd "borrowed" from the office in the barn before someone set it on fire. Most likely, Cici didn't even remember leaving them there.

My burns throbbed, but I ignored them, focusing instead on the pattern emerging from the scattered papers. Equipment failures, lost contracts, mysterious accidents—this was personal. I felt it in my bones.

The wind howled outside, rattling the loose windowpane I'd tried to seal earlier. February in Colorado was always brutal, but tonight, the cold seemed to have an extra bite to it, like nature itself was trying to warn me about what I was uncovering. I pulled my jacket tighter and reached for the thermos of coffee I'd been nursing all morning. The liquid had gone cold hours ago, but I barely noticed. I was too caught up in the story the documents were telling—a story that made my gut twist with every new detail I unveiled.

Four years ago, a promising young bronc threw a shoe during a major competition, leading to a career-ending injury. The timing? Just as the animal was gaining interest for more than bucking. The farrier's report noted unusual wear on the shoe, almost like it had been deliberately weakened. I remembered that horse—a stunning bay stallion named Storm Warning that Hank was particularly proud of. He'd called to tell me about the animal before he placed a bid, explaining the bloodlines that made him a perfect combination of power and control.

"This one's going to change everything," Hank had said. "Bring Morris Ranch to the top of broncs, where it belongs."

While the horse would recover, he wouldn't be able to compete again. And while he could still be bred, he hadn't been on the circuit long, which meant he hadn't yet gained much of a reputation. The traction Hank had hoped for wasn't meant to be. The loss had hit him hard, both financially and personally.

I'd happened to be at the event when the accident took place, watching the color drain from his face as he spoke to the vet. Now, I'd bet anything someone had gotten to that horse before the competition.

Then, three years ago, a trailer axle had snapped on the way to Fort Worth, forcing Hank to default on a contract that would have helped put them in the national spotlight. The maintenance logs showed regular inspections, so the failure made no sense, given the relatively new equipment.

And now, the fire just as I was pushing for the Houston bid. The timing was too perfect to be a coincidence. Someone was making sure Morris Ranch stayed down, and they were getting bolder with each attack.

I took a break when I got a message from Thorn saying he was about to arrive and that Bullet, Stetson, and three other hands who had been brought on to help at the Roaring Fork after Cord had to leave were right behind him.

"Hey, guys. Thanks for being here," I said, meeting them near the ranch house when they pulled in and parked. I'd hoped to introduce them to Cici, but I didn't see her truck where it usually sat out front.

"What've you got for us?" Thorn asked, looking over the barn that had suffered enough damage in the fire that it would probably be cheaper and easier to build a new one.

Before that could be done, an arson investigation would have to be completed, which meant a delay with any insurance settlement. There was room in the south barn for now, but for Morris Ranch to make a go of roughstocking, they were going to have to add more bulls and broncs, which there now wouldn't be enough space for.

"Come with me, and I'll go over it with you." I motioned for all the guys to follow me into the north bunkhouse. "This place is pretty rough, so cleaning it up would be on the list if any of you plan to stay on here."

"I talked to Martinez, who said the southern bunkhouse is in better shape, and there'd be room for us there," said Bullet.

"Good decision," I said, chuckling.

"You might want to consider relocating too," said Stetson as his gaze took in the interior of the building that should probably be replaced when the barn was. To do that, though, would take money Cici didn't have.

My reasons for staying in this one were, first and foremost, because it was where Cici wanted me to stay. Second was its close proximity to the ranch house. There was no way I'd move anywhere where I couldn't see it from one of the windows.

"The list is long and nowhere near complete," I said, handing it to Thorn. "We'll start with getting the fences repaired since it's vital and also inexpensive. As far as any capital for improvements, we'll have to take those on a case-by-case basis."

"Understood." He set the list on the table, making notes, then assigning teams to get started.

"I can't thank you enough for this," I said, turning to each of the men and extending my hand when Thorn indicated they were ready to head out.

"Happy to help out," Stetson muttered, shifting on his feet.

I chuckled, figuring he was anxious to get outside in the fresh air. "Go on, now, and get to work."

However, when the others filed through the door, he didn't.

"What's up, Stet?" I asked.

"Listen, Mr. Wheaton, there's something you need to know. Your brother didn't think it would be a problem, but…"

"Go on."

"It was years ago—hell, Cici and I were babies—but apparently, my pa and Mr. Morris had a falling out."

"Over?"

"Based on what I've been able to piece together from stories the older ranch hands have told, they were roughstocking partners in the late nineties, when rodeo really started to explode in popularity. My pa knew a lot more about horses, and Mr. Morris was better with the bulls."

"With you so far."

"Some say Morris got heavy-handed, wanting everything done his way. Which made sense because then it was the bulls getting all the attention. But you knew my father. He wanted to be in charge, saying the horses brought in more money historically."

This was the first I'd heard about a partnership or a falling out. Both men had always been well-liked and respected in the rodeo industry as well as the local community.

"I'm surprised I never heard anything about it."

Stetson shrugged. "Ancient history, I guess. Unless you're a Hamilton or a Morris."

"What came of it?" I asked.

"They decided to split up, and each developed their own roughstocking programs. When my dad started making inroads with the bulls, Morris accused him of taking credit for things that he came up with."

"Stetson, you said yourself this is ancient history, so why bring it up now?"

"I can't speak for how it was for Cici and Maverick, but we knew better than to ever mention Morris Ranch around my dad. I just don't want anyone thinking that me or my family have anything to do with some of the stuff that's been happening around here."

"Let me ask you this. Do you have a personal beef with the Morris family?"

"No, sir."

It hadn't occurred to me to clear it with Cici before asking for help from the Roaring Fork, and maybe I should have. "We'll talk it over, and if there's an issue, I'll let you know. I doubt there will be."

After he thanked me and left, I sat down at the table and tried to make sense of the reports I was looking at when the sound of my phone buzzing broke my concentration. Another message from Cord. *Any progress?* he asked.

I typed back a quick response. *Working on it.*

Buck said there's a crew from RF on their way.

Already here.

Sorry I can't be of help, bro.

I didn't respond. Telling him how much I needed him more than anyone else would only make him feel worse about a situation neither he nor I could control. Not to mention that, when he'd needed me, I sure as hell wasn't there for him.

The worst of my suspicions didn't have as much to do with what I now saw as the systematic destruction of what Hank Morris had built, as it did with the accident that took his life and Lillian's. My gut was telling me it wasn't a matter of fate that they were on that icy road that night. And that meant Cici might be in far worse straits than the bank threatening foreclosure. Her and Mav's lives might be in danger.

I leaned against the chair, but sat up when it creaked as though it might break to pieces. Rubbing my eyes, I got back to work. Pulling out a fresh legal pad, I started organizing the incidents chronologically. The first signs of trouble had started in earnest a few years ago—small things at first that were easily dismissed. Two years before Hank and Lillian died, things began escalating.

The question that kept nagging at me was why? The land itself was valuable, sure, but there were easier ways to force a sale than this drawn-out campaign of destruction. This felt like whoever was behind it wanted to watch the ranch die slowly, wanted Mav and Cici's parents to feel every loss.

Now, it was Cici they were toying with, letting her think each setback was her fault.

"Fuck," I muttered under my breath, thinking about Stetson saying his father and Hank had had a falling out. I couldn't imagine Bronc Hamilton, as everyone had called him for so long I didn't even know his first name, resorting to the kind of shit going on here. Plus, he'd died shortly after Hank and Lillian did. No way Stetson was behind any of this. That, I was certain of.

I closed my eyes, remembering the look on Cici's face this morning when she'd signed the Houston contract—determination warring with defeat. She blamed herself for everything that had gone wrong since her parents' death, and someone was counting on that self-doubt to break her.

My chest tightened at the thought. She'd already lost so much—her parents, her brother's future, her trust in the world. And here I was, adding to her burden by my mere presence. But even if I could leave, I wouldn't. Someone had to help her, and who better than a man who'd once loved her with his whole heart?

I shook my head and looked over toward the window. Who was I kidding? I'd never stopped loving Cici. I'd only accepted that, now, something that would utterly destroy her if she learned the truth stood between us. Worse, I couldn't imagine what it would do to the seventeen-year-old kid whose secret I'd vowed to keep.

I flipped through more records, looking for anything that might point to who had the access and knowledge to pull this off.

Hours later, after the day got away from me, I realized the sun had set and I'd barely moved from where I sat.

My eyes burned from the strain, but the feeling of dread in my stomach hurt far worse. This wasn't just about destroying the ranch—it was about isolating it. Each loss of a contract or a business relationship had pushed Morris Ranch further to the margins of the industry.

A sound outside pulled me from my thoughts. I got up and saw someone moving between the outbuildings, trying to stay in the shadows, where the bright moonlight wouldn't shine on them. I killed the lamp, staying far enough away to not be seen in the window through which I'd first spotted them.

The figure was dressed in black, moving with purpose toward the equipment barn. Something metallic glinted in their hand—tools or maybe something worse.

Whoever it was navigated their way like they knew the layout by heart, avoiding the motion-sensor lights with practiced ease.

I grabbed my coat from the hook by the door, then my gun from the small kitchen cupboard where I kept it, checking the clip out of habit before tucking it into my waistband. Normally, I didn't believe in mixing bullets and ranch work, but after the fire, I wasn't taking chances. I slipped out the rear door rather than the front, using the skills I'd learned while tracking wild horses to move silently through the snow, keeping my distance as I followed him all the way to the south barn.

When he eased the alley door open just enough to slip inside, I did the same from the side entrance. My eyes adjusted slowly to the darkness. The barn was full of shadows and blind spots, perfect places for someone to hide. I moved cautiously, staying close to the walls, where the floorboards were less likely to creak. A soft scraping sound came from the back corner, where the main stock trailer was kept. It was darker in that area, but my eyes adjusted at the same time the guy was about to duck behind a tractor. I lunged forward, but he was faster, knocking over a stack of empty barrels that crashed between us.

I heard a curse—definitely male, though the voice was too muffled to identify—and the sound of boots on concrete. The intruder knew exactly where the closest exit was, hitting it at full speed while I was still trying to navigate around the fallen barrels.

By the time I made it outside, he was gone, leaving only footprints in the snow. I followed them until they disappeared at the property line, where fresh tire tracks told their own story. Heavy-duty all-terrain tires, probably on a truck or SUV, but they were worn to the point where they should be replaced. The boots were square-toe, which were common. The only other clue, the professional-grade tools used, could very well belong to the ranch. The most important point of information was that this was someone with time to plan these attacks thoroughly.

I studied the impressions left in the mud, memorizing every detail in case the photos I took with my cell didn't show them well enough.

The snow around the vehicle had melted, indicating the engine was probably left running. The man who did this had planned his escape route with a great deal of thought, choosing a spot hidden from both the house and the ranch's security cameras. The ones Kaleb had said didn't appear to be entirely functional anyway.

I returned to the barn and found what he'd been working on—the main hydraulic line on the stock trailer had been partially severed, weakened just enough to fail catastrophically once the trailer was loaded. The cut was precise, done by someone who knew exactly where to strike to cause maximum damage.

A thorough inspection revealed more sabotage— the brake lines had been nicked, the electrical system tampered with, and the hitch mechanism loosened just enough to create play in the connection. If I hadn't interrupted the asshole, we would have lost more than just animals when that trailer failed. The image of Cici or Maverick being anywhere near it when it gave way made my blood run cold.

The discovery left me shaken in a way that had nothing to do with the frigid February night. Someone was willing to risk lives to achieve their goal. The question was, how far would they go? The fire had been bad enough, but this was attempted murder, plain and simple.

I pulled out my phone to document the sabotage, photographing every point of damage. My finger hovered over Kaleb's number, but I stopped short of calling him before I was certain I had enough for him to investigate.

Instead, I spent the next hour checking every piece of equipment in the barn, documenting each instance of potential tampering I found. The pattern was clever, subtle. Small things that could be written off as normal wear and tear until you saw them all together. Whoever was doing this understood machinery, understood how to make accidents look natural, and also got that months could go by without the need for a certain tractor or hay baler. By compromising different things, the odds of injury—or worse—happening sooner multiplied.

The list of suspects would be short. Former employees, competitors, maybe someone from the rodeo circuit who had a grudge against the Morris family. But none of those explained the personal nature of the attacks or the timing that seemed designed to inflict the maximum damage.

Who in the hell would have it out to this extent for a young woman and her teenage brother, who'd lost their parents two years ago? It would take an evil far worse than what I'd seen in my life to destroy an entire family. I wondered if Cici would have any idea, or had whatever suspicion there might have been gotten buried when her parents were?

By the time I finished my inspection, it was close to seven-thirty. My body ached from hours of little sleep, followed by too much time spent in the cold barn, but my mind was racing too fast to rest. I gathered all the evidence I'd collected—photos, documents, notes— which, once I returned to the bunkhouse, I'd secure in the false bottom of my duffel bag.

Along the way, I thought over everything I'd learned. The sabotage, the financial manipulation, the escalating violence—it all pointed to someone with a deep understanding of both the ranch operations and the family itself. Someone patient enough to play a long game, smart enough to cover their tracks, and ruthless enough to risk lives to achieve their goal.

All of that added up to one thing—the kind of knowledge and access that only came from years of close contact.

Tomorrow, I'd see if I could get a list of everyone who'd worked the ranch in the past ten years. Ranch hands came and went, but the person or people behind this had to have been around longer. Someone whose loyalty to the Morris family had either been broken or bought.

I stopped and looked over at the house, where I wondered if Cici and Maverick were finished having dinner, unaware of just how much danger they were in.

The sun had long since set, but the moon's glow bathed the snow in a soothing color that felt like a lie. Somewhere out there, someone was planning their next move. Someone who wouldn't stop until Morris Ranch was destroyed and the family along with it.

God, I wanted a drink. Needed one.

Movement from the house caught my attention as I trekked to the bunkhouse. Cici's bedroom light clicked on as she ended her day. I watched her shadow move across the window and made a silent promise to both her and her father that I would find who was behind this, no matter what it cost me personally.

Because the alternative was too much to imagine. I had to do this. Save the ranch and, by extension, her and Maverick. And that meant I couldn't give in to the temptation of alcohol. I had to stay sober.

Kaleb was probably out with friends after a long shift, or on a date, or maybe he'd even called it a night and was sound asleep. I was about to stuff the phone in my pocket when I heard his voice in my head, telling me that whenever I felt like I couldn't resist ending my sobriety, I should call him. That it didn't matter what time, day or night. All that mattered was that I did not take that drink.

I dug out my phone and placed the call.

6

Cici

I watched my brother withdraw further into himself with each passing day. The confident, energetic kid who used to light up a room had been replaced by someone I barely recognized. His mood swings were getting worse, and the isolation wasn't helping. After finding another empty bottle of Jack hidden under his bed—our dad's brand—I couldn't ignore the signs anymore.

The kitchen was quiet except for the scrape of Mav's fork against his plate. He'd barely touched his food, pushing the meatloaf around like a sullen child instead of the almost-man he was supposed to be. Dark circles shadowed his eyes, matching the ones I saw in the mirror every morning.

The recipe was one of Mav's favorites of our mom's—one of the few things of hers I could still get right—but lately, even comfort food wasn't enough to get him to eat.

The kitchen smelled of onions, red peppers, and mushrooms—Mom's secret ingredients. She'd taught me how to make her signature dish one rainy Sunday, both of us laughing when I made a mess of the breadcrumbs. "Cooking with love means getting your hands dirty," she'd said. Now, I followed her instructions like a ritual, as if getting each step perfect might somehow bring back those easier days.

"You need to eat," I said, trying to keep my voice gentle despite the worry gnawing at my gut.

He shrugged, a gesture so reminiscent of our father that it made my chest ache. "Not hungry."

"Mav—"

"Don't." His fork clattered against the plate. "Don't use that tone. The one that sounds exactly like Mom when she was about to lecture us."

The comparison stung, mostly because he was right. I'd been trying so hard to fill the void our parents left that sometimes I forgot I was his sister first. "I found another bottle."

His face went blank—another habit he'd picked up recently. "So?"

"So, you're seventeen. And mixing alcohol, that you aren't old enough to even have, with your pain meds—"

"I'm fine." He pushed back from the table. "The meds barely help anyway."

"Then, we'll talk to Dr. Mitchell about adjusting them." I reached for his arm, but he jerked away.

"What's the point? My leg's never going to be the same. Might as well accept it like everyone else has."

The bitterness in his voice cut deep. "That's not true. The physical therapy—"

"Is a waste of time." His laugh was harsh and empty as he smacked his thigh. "I can't even remember how it happened. Just woke up in the hospital with everyone telling me—" His jaw clenched when he stopped himself.

"Telling you what?" My pulse quickened, already knowing he wouldn't continue. He never did when the conversation turned to that night.

"Nothing." He grabbed his crutches, the movement too fast, too desperate. "I'm tired. Going to bed."

"It's only eight."

"Then, I'm going to my room to stare at the ceiling and think about all the things I'll never do. Better?"

I watched him hobble away, each uneven step a reminder of everything we'd lost. The sound of his door slamming echoed through the house—a house that felt too big, too empty, too full of ghosts and secrets.

The floorboards creaked under his uneven gait, a sound that had become as familiar as breathing. Before the accident, he used to take the stairs two at a time, always in a rush to get somewhere, do something. Now, each step was measured, careful, like he was afraid of falling.

The kitchen seemed to close in around me as I cleaned up, my muscle memory taking over while my mind raced. Mom used to say the kitchen was the heart of a home, but lately, it felt more like a museum of what we'd lost. Her copper-bottom pots still hung in the same order she'd kept them. Dad's coffee mug— the chipped one with the bad joke about cowboys—sat in its spot by the maker, untouched since that night. I thought about washing it once, but couldn't bring myself to erase the coffee ring beneath it—the last thing he'd left behind.

Knowing sleep was a long way off, I pulled out the ranch's ledgers, but instead of diving into the numbers, I found myself drawn to the photos stuck between the pages. Our dad showing Mav how to rope when he was barely big enough to hold the lariat. Mom teaching me to read a horse's body language, her patience infinite as I struggled to understand. Family snapshots that felt like artifacts from another life.

A particularly loud gust of wind rattled the windows, drawing my attention outside. Porter was crossing the yard toward the equipment barn, his stride purposeful even at this hour. It wasn't late, but the workday had ended long ago.

Part of me wanted to tell him to get some rest, but that would mean acknowledging I cared about his well-being, and I couldn't afford that kind of weakness.

Still, I found myself watching him disappear into one of the outbuildings. He'd been working nonstop since the fire, taking on tasks I hadn't even known needed to be done. It was getting harder to hold on to my anger when his every action seemed focused on saving what was left of my family's legacy.

The sound of breaking glass upstairs shattered my thoughts. I took the stairs two at a time, my heart pounding. "Mav?"

No answer. I tried his door—locked.

"Maverick! Open up!"

Silence, then a muffled curse followed by retching sounds.

I didn't hesitate. The old bobby pin I kept in my pocket made quick work of the lock—a trick Dad had taught me. The scene inside knocked the breath from my lungs.

Mav was hunched over his trash can, the broken remnants of another whiskey bottle scattered across the floor. The smell of alcohol and vomit filled the air. His room was a mess of tangled sheets and discarded clothes, pain medication bottles lined up on his night-stand like silent accusers.

His rodeo trophies still lined the shelves, collecting dust now. Junior championships, buckles he'd won before he could drive—evidence of the future he'd been building. I'd offered to pack them away once, but the look he gave me had stopped that conversation cold. Some wounds were still too fresh to touch.

"Let me help," I said softly, picking my way through the broken glass.

"Go away." His voice was raw, defeated. "Just…go away, Cici."

Instead, I helped him clean up and get into bed, ignoring his weak protests. He was asleep before I fin-ished picking up the glass, his face finally peaceful in a way it never was when he was awake.

Back in the kitchen, I sat down, knowing I didn't have the energy to review the ledgers but also that if I went to bed, I'd just lie there, worrying.

A knock on the door made me jump. Juan Martinez, a ranch hand who'd worked for us since before my parents died, stood there, looking uncomfortable. "Miss Morris? Sorry to bother you so late, but there's something you should see in the west pasture."

I followed him out into the night, the wind cutting through my jacket. The beam of his flashlight swept across the ground, illuminating fresh tire tracks just outside our fence line. Beside them, something metallic gleamed in the darkness—shell casings.

"Found them while doing my evening checks," Martinez said quietly. "Look fresh."

I crouched down, my fingers hovering over the brass cylinders. They were indeed fresh, probably from today. Someone had been on our property, armed. What bothered me the most was that I hadn't heard any gunshots. Why not? What about Mav or Porter? Had they?

"You said you found them while doing evening checks? Are you always out working this late?"

He shook his head. "Sorry, I was gone most of the day on a personal matter."

"It's okay," I muttered, thinking about my dad again when the brass caught the moonlight, reminding me of the way he used to check his own shells before heading out to deal with predators. He'd had a sixth sense about threats to the ranch. "Trust your gut," he'd say, "but verify with your eyes." Right now, both my gut and my eyes were screaming that something was very wrong.

The threatening letters stuffed in my desk drawer suddenly felt more real, more dangerous.

"Don't tell Mr. Wheaton," I said, surprising myself with the order. "Not yet."

Martinez nodded, but I caught the doubt in his expression. I couldn't deal with that now, though. Whatever decisions I made had to be based on what I thought was best for my brother and me.

Once back at the house, I heard Mav moving around upstairs, probably searching for another bottle he thought I didn't know about. I'd say I'd fire whichever ranch hand was helping my underage brother get his hands on alcohol, but it could literally be anyone. Hard drinking was part of the "cowboy way of life." Anyone who didn't know that had never set foot on a ranch.

I rubbed the back of my neck as the weight of everything—our roughstock struggles, my brother's pain, Porter's mysterious arrival, and now, armed trespassers who'd fired shots I hadn't heard—pressed down on me until I could barely breathe.

The ranch was more than just land and livestock—it was the story of my family written in fence posts and bloodlines. Every corner held a memory—the round pen where Dad had taught me to gentle wild horses, the creek where Mom had showed me how to find arrowheads after spring floods, the oak tree Mav fell from when he was ten, swearing he could fly. The tack room still held my dad's training journals, leather-bound books filled with his careful observations about each horse that passed through our gates.

I'd found myself reading them lately, trying to understand not just his methods with horses, but his thoughts about the ranch's future. The last entry was dated three days before the accident, the pen strokes rushed like he'd been distracted.

Now, those memories were tangled up with newer, darker ones. The north barn, for which I didn't yet know the full extent of the damage. The empty bottles under Mav's bed. The shadow of Porter Wheaton moving through spaces that used to belong only to us.

I pulled Dad's old shotgun from the closet and checked the loads—a habit he'd drilled into me that seemed more necessary with each passing day. The shell casings in the west pasture meant someone was watching us, waiting. But for what?

The light in the equipment barn finally went dark. I watched Porter's figure move through the moonlight toward the bunkhouse, his steps heavy with what I assumed was exhaustion. At some point tomorrow, I'd have to face him and pretend I didn't see him checking on things day and night when he thought I wasn't looking.

Just like I pretended I didn't notice how my brother retreated further into himself with each passing day.

I stepped outside, breathing in the night air that carried the scent of snow. That crisp, clean smell always reminded me of better times—weekend rides with Dad, Mom's hot chocolate waiting when we got back, Mav's laughter echoing across the yard. Now, it just felt like another layer of cold, another reminder of how much we'd lost and how much more we stood to lose.

Standing guard over my broken family, I realized time might not be on our side. Something was happening to the ranch—to all of us—and I couldn't shake the feeling that it was only going to get worse before it got better. If there was still a chance for better, at all. Another thing my dad used to say was that hope was like a good horse—you had to work to maintain it, train it, and believe in it even when it fought you. These days, hope felt more like a wild thing, slipping through my fingers no matter how tightly I tried to hold on.

7

Porter

I woke just before six, my body clock refusing to let me sleep later even though I'd only managed a few hours of rest. The bunkhouse was freezing—the ancient wood stove had gone out sometime during the night. I pulled on my boots and jacket, knowing there were more reports for me to review before starting the day's work.

The records painted a grim picture. Years of thoughtful decisions were being undone by necessity and crisis. I understood why Cici had made the choices she had—when you're drowning, you grab whatever lifeline you can reach. But selling off key bloodlines had created a genetic bottleneck that would take an equal amount of time to correct.

A knock at the door startled me. I hadn't heard any-one approach, which was unusual, given the crunch of snow that normally gave away visitors. When I opened it, Cici stood there, wringing her gloved hands.

"Thought you might want breakfast," she said, her tone free of inflection. "Up at the house."

The invitation caught me off guard. In the three days I'd been here, I made an effort to respect Cici's boundaries by keeping my distance from the main house unless it was absolutely necessary to stop in. "You sure?"

She nodded once. "The kitchen's warm."

I followed her across the yard, watching how she moved through the familiar space with unconscious grace. The morning light caught her dark hair, turning the loose strands to fire. I forced myself to look away.

The kitchen was indeed warm, and the smell of coffee and bacon wrapped around me like the memory of my own kitchen, back when my mom was still alive. She had the same copper pots Cici's mom had. Like ours, theirs looked less polished now.

"Martinez found shell casings by the west fence last night," she blurted, pouring coffee into two mugs.

My hand froze halfway to the cup. "What caliber?"

"You don't seem surprised."

"Should I be?" I kept my voice steady, not mentioning the sabotaged equipment I'd discovered or my suspicions about her parents' accident.

She pushed a plate of eggs toward me. "A few days ago, someone left a note. 'Sell or suffer.'" Her laugh was bitter. "Real creative, right?"

"Why didn't you tell me?"

"Why should I have?" Her eyes met mine, challenging. "You're not exactly forthcoming yourself."

Before I could respond, my phone buzzed. The text was from the event organizers in Fort Worth, saying they needed stock for a competition in five days. It was a prestigious opportunity, one that could help rebuild Morris Ranch's reputation. But the timing would take me away for longer than forty-eight hours. The trust's requirements echoed in my head: no absences longer than that or my siblings and I would lose everything. More importantly, the ranch didn't have stock ready for an event like this one.

"Bad news?" Cici asked when I set the phone down without responding.

"No, just…complicated." I took a sip of coffee to buy time. "Speaking of complicated, we need to talk about RodeoHouston. The stock's not ready yet."

"Yet you pushed me to sign the contract anyway."

"Because we can get them ready. But we'll need help." I thought of Matt Rice, whose family owned the

Flying R Ranch in Crested Butte. His father had been supplying stock for major events since before I was born. Matt took over after his dad retired and had probably forgotten more about roughstocking than most contractors would ever know.

We'd partnered in several high-profile events in the last few years, and if asked, I knew he'd help. He owed me one after I'd stepped in at the last minute at the National Finals Rodeo two seasons ago, when his stock manager broke his leg. Even if he didn't owe me, he'd do whatever he could anyway.

Having Thorn here was a huge help. Especially given he never seemed flustered by anything. The guy was the calmest, most easygoing I'd ever met. Which might also mean he buried whatever shit was in his life as deep as the rest of us did. Bullet and Stetson were assets too, which reminded me that later, I'd need to talk to Cici about him being here.

As far as other outside support, I knew Decker Ashford would set Morris Ranch up with a top-of-the-line security system. The man had revolutionized ranch protection after a series of high-profile livestock thefts hit the circuit. I'd heard he owned another company that did government-type work that was worth billions, but he'd never forgotten his ranching roots. One call, and he'd have a team out here within days, probably at no cost once he understood the situation.

The shell casings Martinez had found made the call to Ashford more urgent than ever. After breakfast, it would be one of the first things I'd do.

After I ticked that off the list, I'd call my brothers. Buck had extensive construction expertise, not to mention he was a former intelligence officer who'd worked for Ashford. Holt, who was typically somewhere in the world, touring with the band CB Rice, would step up too if he was around. The thought of my younger brother's music made me smile; his songs had gotten me through some dark nights when the urge to drink nearly won.

"What are you thinking about?" Cici's voice pulled me from my thoughts.

"My family." The admission came easily, surprising me.

Her expression softened slightly. "Must be hard being away from them."

I shrugged, not trusting myself to speak. The guilt of potentially costing them everything was what really weighed heavily.

"I know someone who could help with security upgrades—" I started.

"We can't afford—"

"Cost isn't an issue." The words came out before I could stop them.

"Why?" Her eyes narrowed and bored into mine. "Why are you really here, Porter?"

The secrets I kept pressed down hard on me—Maverick's accident, the trust requirements, my suspicions about the sabotage. I thought about telling her everything, but the memory of her brother's haunted eyes that night stopped me. "I'm where I want to be."

The moment stretched between us, filled with things I couldn't say. Then Maverick's uneven steps sounded on the stairs, followed by the unmistakable smell of whiskey. When he appeared in the doorway, his eyes were bloodshot, his movements unsteady.

"Mornin'," he mumbled, surprisingly gentle despite his obvious intoxication. There was something in the way he looked at me—not with hatred or anger, more like confusion, maybe even gratitude. It made the guilt churn harder in my stomach.

"Mav," Cici's voice was sharp with worry. "It's not even ten in the morning."

"Don't start." He grabbed the counter for balance. "Not today, okay?"

I stood slowly. "I should go."

"You don't have to," Maverick said, his words slurring. "Looks like Ceec made breakfast."

Something in his tone made my chest ache. Here was a kid, fighting demons he couldn't even remember. I'd promised him that night, when he was barely conscious and begging me not to tell his sister, that I'd protect him. And I would keep that promise, no matter the cost to me. Still, watching him struggle now was painful to witness.

I wanted to tell him about that night, about his desperate plea that I still honored. About how none of this was my burden to bear, but I chose to carry it because he'd asked me to. Because, sometimes, protecting people meant making hard choices.

"Another time," I said quietly. "Thanks for breakfast, Cici," I added, even though I hadn't eaten more than a couple of bites.

I heard them arguing as I left—Cici's worried tone, Maverick's defensive responses. Their voices followed me across the yard, reminding me of all the ways I'd failed my own family.

When I went inside, ranch work waited on the bunkhouse table that had become my temporary desk, but I couldn't focus on it. Instead, I found myself thinking about the similarities between Maverick's struggle and my own battle with alcohol. I knew the signs and recognized the desperation in his eyes. Part of me wanted to reach out, to tell him about my own journey to sobriety, about how Kaleb had helped me through those first brutal days. How he'd helped me just last night.

But I wasn't his friend or his mentor. I was the man keeping his secret, the man his sister blamed because that was exactly what I'd agreed to let happen. Any attempt to help would only complicate an already impossible situation.

Still, watching him spiral hit too close to home. I pulled out my phone, thumb hovering over Kaleb's number for the second time in less than twenty-four hours. My friend and AA sponsor, and the only other person who knew what really happened that night, might be able to find a way to get through to Maverick.

But no, that would be another deception, another manipulation. First, the kid needed to acknowledge his problem and want to do something about it. No one could force him into it.

I tried to focus on the papers strewn about on my table, but my mind kept drifting back to Maverick. The trust requirements meant I had to stay here and watch him struggle. But maybe that was the real challenge—not the year of confinement.

I stood near the window, but the morning sun did nothing to warm the cold certainty in my gut when I thought about the mounting evidence that someone was willing to kill to get what they wanted.

I returned to the table and opened my laptop, determined to lose myself in work. The roughstock program needed an overhaul, the security systems needed upgrading, and the equipment needed repairs. These were problems I could solve, unlike so many other things in my life.

But first, I had to figure out how to handle the event request. Three days away would violate the trust's requirements, potentially costing my family everything. Yet, turning it down might cost Morris Ranch a crucial opportunity for redemption. Then again, we weren't ready.

Another knock at my door pulled me from my thoughts. This time, when I opened it, Cici stood there holding a big basket wrapped in a towel.

"Peace offering," she said. "I shouldn't have let things get heated earlier."

"Let me get that for you," I offered, stepping back to let her in.

I set the basket on a chair, then grabbed the mess of papers on the table. While I took them into the bedroom, Cici unpacked what she'd brought.

When I returned, steam rose from two cups of coffee she'd poured, and the smell of homemade biscuits and bacon filled the small space.

"Tell me about the Roaring Fork," she said as we dug into the food she brought. "What were you building there?"

The question surprised me. "A well-rounded roughstock program, focusing mainly on bucking bulls with specific traits—more athlete than outlaw." I took a sip of coffee, remembering my pride in what we'd accomplished. "We'd just started seeing results when..." I trailed off, not wanting to mention either the accident or the trust that had brought me here.

"Dad talked about your program sometimes." She broke a biscuit in half, studying it rather than looking at me. "He admired what you were doing. Said you understood bloodlines in a way most people didn't."

"He taught me most of what I know." The admission came easily. "Everything else I learned, trying to live up to his standards."

"Why did you give it up?" Her eyes met mine. "Why come here when you have something of your own?"

I set my coffee down, weighing how much to tell her and taking a deep breath before I spoke. "Cici, I made a promise to your father. If anything ever happened to him, I'd make sure his family was taken care of."

"You what?"

"It was the last time I saw him. He was worried about something, though he wouldn't say what. Made me swear I'd look out for you, your mom, and Maverick." I swallowed hard. "I never thought…"

Cici's hands trembled, and she set down her coffee. "I was at school at Western State when it happened," she said softly. "I got a call in the middle of the night.

By the time I made it home…" She shook her head. "Dad was always so careful about road conditions, especially with Mom in the car. He'd cancel major meetings if the weather was bad enough. It never made sense that they'd go out in a storm like that. Nothing was worth that kind of risk to him."

Her words stirred something in me. Hank Morris, who'd built his reputation on careful, calculated decisions, inexplicably took a fatal risk.

"Porter?" Cici's voice pulled me back. "You went somewhere just now."

"Just thinking." I couldn't tell her my suspicions yet, not without proof. "Your dad was a smart man. He must have had a reason."

"You know what's strange?" She wrapped her arms around herself. "Their accident happened almost exactly where Mav's did. Same curve, same guardrail." She noticed my reaction and misread it. "I'm sorry, I didn't say that to make you feel—"

The rest of her words faded as blood rushed in my ears. Same curve. Same guardrail. The pieces started shifting in my mind, forming a picture I didn't want to see.

A loud crack from outside made us both jump. Through the window, I caught a glimpse of movement by the equipment barn.

"Stay here," I said, reaching for my coat and gun.

But Cici was already on her feet. "Like hell, I will."

I grabbed her arm as another crack split the air—this one unmistakably from a firearm.

"Mav!" she gasped, face going pale. "He was heading to check the back pasture."

The horror in her voice mirrored what I felt as we both raced out of the bunkhouse.

8

Cici

The gunshots sent my heart into my throat. Porter and I raced across the frozen ground, our breath coming in white clouds in the frigid air. The pasture was shrouded in shadows, making it impossible to see more than a few feet ahead. Then I heard a groan that made my blood run cold.

"Oh my God!" I spotted Jack Shaw, who'd worked for our family for years, slumped against a fence, one hand pressed to his shoulder. Even in the dim light, I could see blood seeping between his fingers.

Porter reached him first, already shrugging out of his coat. "Let me see." His voice was steady, authoritative. He pressed his wadded-up coat against the wound while I dropped to my knees beside them.

"Caught someone…messing with the fence," Shaw managed through gritted teeth. "Couldn't see their face. They fired twice and ran."

"We need to get him to the hospital." Porter's eyes met mine. "My truck keys are hanging by the door in the bunkhouse. It's closer, and it's got four-wheel drive."

I nodded and took off running. When I reached the bunkhouse, what I saw made me stumble to a halt. A piece of paper had been nailed to the wood in the few minutes we were with Shaw. My hands shook as I pulled it free.

"Leave now, or the next shot won't miss," it read in words that had been cut from magazines, just like the other notes and letters I'd received.

But this one was different—it targeted Porter specifically. My chest tightened. Someone had been watching us, had seen him becoming essential to the ranch's recovery. Maybe even saw him becoming important to me in a way I'd never anticipated could happen again.

I grabbed the key fob and shoved the note in my pocket, trying to ignore how the thought of Porter leaving—by choice or by force—made my stomach twist. We needed him. The ranch needed him. I wasn't ready to examine why that terrified me more than the threat itself.

When I returned, Porter had already helped Shaw to his feet. The wound was a graze, but there was enough blood to turn my stomach. I unlocked the vehicle and helped him get Shaw in the rear seat, then climbed in beside him.

"Keep pressure on it," Porter instructed after I'd handed him the key fob and he started the engine. "Jack, you still with us?"

"Yeah, I'm still kickin'," Shaw grunted. "Been better, but I've also been worse."

I studied his face. Jack had taught me to drive a stick shift and, along with my father, helped Mav learn to rope. Now, here he was, bleeding because someone wanted to destroy everything our family had built.

"Who would do this?" I whispered, more to myself than anyone.

"Someone who knows the ranch," Shaw said, his voice tight with pain. "They knew exactly where to wait. Knew my routines."

Porter's eyes met mine in the rearview mirror. I could see him processing this information, adding it to whatever mental catalog he was keeping of the ranch's troubles. I should tell him about the other notes, I realized. About all the little things that hadn't added up even before he arrived.

But not now. Not with Shaw bleeding in my arms and the sun shining on a ranch that felt more like a battlefield with each passing day.

At the hospital, Porter handled everything while I called Kaleb. The sheriff arrived as they were taking Shaw back for treatment. His expression was grim when I told him what happened.

"I'll need statements from all of you," he said, pulling out his notebook. "And I want to check those tracks before they get trampled."

"I should get back," I said, thinking of Mav. "My brother—"

"I called Thorn," Porter cut in. "He's, err, keeping an eye on things. Let me handle this part, Cici. You stay with Shaw," he added when I started to protest.

I shook my head, unable to process what he'd just said. Thorn? Someone was keeping an eye on things? Did he mean at our ranch?

Rather than hurl questions at him, I paused. There was no arrogance in what he'd said, no attempt to take control. Just genuine concern and a steadiness I desperately needed right now.

I waited while Shaw got stitched up, his usual easy smile strained but present. "Been noticing things. I know Juan showed you the shell casings, but there's been more," he admitted when I asked why he'd been checking the fence so early. "Tracks by the old barn before dawn. Equipment moved when it shouldn't be. Didn't want to worry you with everything else going on."

The words hit hard. How many people had been keeping quiet about things they'd seen, trying to protect me? And how many secrets was I still keeping that might get someone else hurt?

"You should tell Porter," I found myself saying. "About the tracks, everything. He needs to know."

Shaw studied me for a long moment. "You're starting to trust him again."

"I don't think I have a choice."

But that wasn't quite true. The real truth was harder to face—I was starting to *want* to trust him. Starting to rely on his steady presence and his unwavering determination to help us. The thought of him leaving filled me with dread. I'd loved Porter Wheaton once. In fact, I thought the day would come when he might ask me to marry him. Instead, he broke my heart.

I shook my head a second time—harder—not wanting to relive that time of my life. My focus needed to be on things like the note in my pocket that felt like it would burn a hole through the fabric. Someone had watched us long enough to know targeting Porter would hurt the ranch. Might even hurt me.

When had that happened? When had Porter Wheaton gone from being the person I blamed for destroying my brother's future to the man I relied on? More, wanted to rely on?

"Your father liked him. He was sad the two of you broke up but smart enough to know he had to stay out of it," Shaw said quietly. "Porter handles things the same way Hank would've. The way he looks at you when you're not watching."

"That was a long time ago. A different life." One when both my parents were alive and Maverick was turning into a promising bull rider. Porter had been at the ranch for a handful of days. Until then, and even after his arrival, I considered him an enemy. That I felt so vulnerable was the only reason my opinion had changed so drastically and so quickly. I wasn't ready for that observation or its implications.

Bert Johnson, who roomed with Shaw in the south bunkhouse, picked the two of us up from the hospital. I'd offered to let Jack recover at the ranch house, but he'd refused, saying he'd be more comfortable in his "own" space. Rather than have them drop me off there, I rode along to help Shaw get settled.

When Bert and I helped him inside, the first thing I noticed was how different it appeared from the north version. I'd known the south one was in much better shape, but seeing it now, after being in the other with Porter earlier, shamed me. I'd sent the man who was helping us, seemingly out of the goodness of his heart after promising my father he would, to stay in a structure on the verge of being uninhabitable. It was something I intended to rectify as soon as I saw him.

When Johnson took me home, I saw Porter's truck parked in front of that rundown bunkhouse, then spotted him talking to Kaleb by the fence where Martinez had found tracks and shell casings.

I pulled the note from my pocket, staring at the crude letters. I should show it to Porter. Should tell him about the others. About all the strange things that had been happening even before he arrived.

But first, I needed to understand why the thought of him leaving felt like losing a piece of myself I'd only just discovered had returned.

I found him back at the bunkhouse later that after-noon, hunched over documents spread across the rickety table. They looked like the same ones he'd gathered and taken into the other room earlier. When I rapped on the partially open door, he looked up with an expression that was best described as neutral. The burns on his arms from the fire were still visible, a reminder of how much he'd already risked for us.

"Shaw settled in?" he asked.

I nodded, lingering in the doorway. "Porter, about you staying here—"

"If you mean in this bunkhouse, don't worry about it. I've slept in worse places."

"That's not the point." I stepped inside, picking up one of the papers he'd been studying. "You shouldn't have to. There's plenty of room in the ranch house."

His head snapped up, and his eyes were wide. "Cici—"

"Please." I met his gaze steadily. "With everything that's happening…I'd feel safer if you were closer."

I watched as his internal struggle played out in his expression—his instinct to maintain a distance warring with his need to protect. When he finally nodded, I let out a breath I hadn't realized I was holding.

"Okay," he said quietly. "If you're sure."

"I am." I set the sheet of paper down. "What are you working on?"

He hesitated only a moment before spreading out several documents. "Looking for patterns. The shooter knew Shaw's schedule, knew exactly where to wait. That kind of knowledge takes time to acquire."

The conversation was interrupted by Kaleb's arrival.

"Found something you both need to see," he said after Porter invited him in.

We followed him out to where Shaw had been shot. The sheriff crouched down to where the fence had been tampered with. "Professional-grade wire cutters. Not to mention, the water lines have been compromised."

"The water lines?"

"They're trying to separate the north pasture from the rest," said Porter. "Cut off the water access."

I felt sick. Without that water source, we'd have to move the entire herd. The cost would be astronomical.

"There's more." Kaleb stood, brushing off his hands. "The shell casings match the ones Martinez found last week. Same shooter."

"Last week?" Porter's voice was sharp. "There were other shots fired?"

This was news to me too. The first I'd heard about were the ones he found last night.

Porter paced in the dirt, his jaw tight with barely contained anger. Not at me, I realized, but at the situation. At the growing web of threats and secrets that seemed to be swirling around us.

"There's more I should've told you," I finally said.

He stopped pacing. "Like what?"

"Other notes I've received."

He studied me but didn't speak right away, perhaps in an effort to control his temper. "Yes, you should've," he finally said, looking from me to the sheriff, then back again. "Have you told Kaleb?"

"No."

He took a deep breath and let it out slowly. "Let's go inside." He motioned for Kaleb and me to follow him.

By the time we reached the bunkhouse's table, I'd pulled the note from my pocket and unfolded it. "I found this earlier when you told me to get your keys."

"Where?" he asked as I handed it to him.

"Nailed to the door."

He looked at it, then handed it to the other man.

"Leave now, or the next shot won't miss," Kaleb read out loud. "Do you think this was for Porter?"

"Why else would it have been nailed to the door of this place?"

Porter walked over to the window, his shoulders tense. "We need to start being honest with each other, Cici. All of us. Before someone gets killed instead of just wounded."

The truth of his words stung, but I agreed. We were all keeping secrets, and like land mines, they were waiting to explode.

"I have the other notes," I admitted. "Ones that came before today's. They're in Dad's desk. I think…I think you need to see them."

Porter turned back to me, his expression unreadable. "Let's go," he said, heading to the door, with Kaleb and me following.

The walk to the house felt longer than usual. Each step was a choice—to trust, to let someone else in, to face possibilities I'd been avoiding. When we reached Dad's office, I pulled out the key I kept on a chain around my neck—the one that opened the bottom drawer, where I'd been collecting evidence of everything that had gone wrong since my parents died.

As I reached for the handle, I realized my hands were shaking. Showing Porter these notes meant letting him see how deep the trouble really went. It meant trusting him with more than just the ranch's future.

If he turned his back on me because of the threats, I wasn't sure what I would do.

"Cici…" he prompted, his eyes boring into mine.

I pulled everything out and set it on the table in front of him and the sheriff, then shut my eyes and prayed.

9

Porter

I spread the papers across Hank's old desk, my stomach churning as I read each threat. The earliest ones were vague—warnings about selling while they could still get a "fair" price. But they escalated quickly. Graphic descriptions of accidents that could befall livestock.

When I saw the photos sent too, they made me want to hit something. They included surveillance shots of Cici doing routine chores—checking fences, working horses, walking into the barns. They captured her quiet determination, but also how isolated and vulnerable she'd become. Whoever took them had gotten close—way too close.

I lowered my arms so my hands were out of view and clenched my fists. Why hadn't she shared any of this?

"The barn fire was threatened here." Cici pointed to a note postmarked two weeks before the blaze. "And Thunder Cloud being hurt…"

"Jesus," I muttered under my breath, studying the photo showing the stallion's usual morning turnout. The timestamp from that day matched when he'd gotten tangled in the rope. Not an accident, after all.

Her hands shook as she spread out maintenance records. "I've been documenting everything. The bigger problems started after Mom and Dad died, but looking back…" She swallowed hard. "There were signs before. Things Dad was worried about."

Soon, I'd need to share all I'd documented too. God knew what she'd do when she realized things were so much worse than even she believed. When my eyes met Kaleb's, he shook his head.

"This is bad, Cici. We need to—"

A commotion outside pulled us from the grim evidence. Through the window, I spotted Johnson running toward the house.

"The north well pump is smoking," he gasped when we met him at the door. "And the backup isn't responding. We've got four hundred head with no water access. I tried to get it running, but there's something wrong with the electrical system."

"How long until the portable tanks run dry?" Cici asked, already heading to the barn.

"Hard to say, but not very long."

I did quick mental calculations. The cattle would start showing signs of serious distress within hours of the water running out. Once dehydration set in, we'd lose control completely. "We need to move them to the south pasture. Now."

"The fences there aren't ready," Cici protested.

"They are. I've had a crew here, working on them."

She opened her mouth, then shut it. Now wasn't the time for us to talk about the things I'd done without consulting her like I'd agreed to.

"Let's go," I said, grabbing my jacket. "Those cattle start getting dehydrated, and we'll have a stampede on our hands. And a lot of dead livestock."

Her jaw clenched and unclenched like my fists had earlier. "Johnson, get Martinez started on the portable tanks. Whatever we can salvage from the north side."

"I'll get Thunder Cloud saddled," I said. "We'll need him to move the herd."

Cici's eyes widened. "You can't—"

"He knows me. And he's the strongest horse you've got." I held her gaze. "Trust me. Just this once."

Something shifted in her expression—fear warring with necessity. Finally, she nodded. "I'll take Stormchaser. She's not as fast, but she's steady."

"I'll help," Kaleb offered. "Point where I need to go."

I raced into the barn, wishing I'd already called Decker Ashford like I planned to, and my brothers.

When I approached Thunder Cloud's stall, the stallion's ears pricked forward at my footsteps, and I took a moment to let him catch my scent. There was so much power in his massive frame, but there was intelligence too. He'd proven that during the fire.

Once he was saddled up, I led him out of the barn and threw a leg over. I increased my calf pressure and clucked. Thunder Cloud danced under me as we sped out of the pasture. It was as though the animal sensed the urgency, sensed I was relying on him. Cici rode beside me on Stormchaser, her face set in determined lines as we approached the restless herd.

The cattle were already showing signs of distress, crowding around the dry tanks. Moving them would be tricky—one spooked animal could start a chain reaction. And someone had deliberately put us in this position.

"Take the left flank. Nice and easy. Let them see us coming," I called to her just as Bullet rode up with three of the other hands.

"We were out east," he hollered. "What's going on?"

"Tanks are dry."

The look in his eyes told me he knew they hadn't just run out of water, but again, now wasn't the time to debate the situation.

"Spread out along the ridge. Don't let any break away toward the north fence," I said to Bullet, who nodded.

Cici followed me, guiding Stormchaser wide, realizing we'd need to push them through a narrow gate, then along a quarter mile of fence line before reaching the south pasture. One wrong move, and all hell would break loose.

The first cow moved, then another. Thunder Cloud responded to the slightest pressure, helping turn the herd. For a moment, I thought we might actually pull this off easier than I'd anticipated.

Then a shot cracked across the pasture.

The herd exploded into motion. Cattle scattered in every direction, bellowing in panic. Thunder Cloud reared, but I kept my seat, already scanning for the shooter. The sound had come from the tree line to the east, where shadows still clung to the underbrush. Wasn't that where Bullet said he'd been working?

"Cici!" I shouted, spinning around in time to see her struggling to control Stormchaser as cattle surged around them. Without thinking, I spurred Thunder Cloud toward them.

When we heard another shot—closer this time—a bull broke from the herd, heading straight for Cici. I saw the moment Stormchaser lost her footing in a gopher hole, then Cici start to fall.

Thunder Cloud responded instantly to my commands, cutting through the stampeding cattle. I reached Cici just as she hit the ground, hauling her up behind me as the bull charged past. Her arms wrapped around my waist instinctively, and I felt her whole body trembling.

"Hold on!" I yelled over the chaos. Thunder Cloud pivoted, facing the scattered herd. The stallion seemed to understand exactly what we needed, moving with perfect precision to cut off escaping animals.

Working as one, we managed to turn the cattle back toward the gate. Her body pressed against my back, her breath warm on my neck as she called directions. Every point of contact felt like electricity, but I forced myself to focus on the task at hand. Thorn, Stetson, and the third hand appeared on the ridge, helping funnel the terrified animals.

It took nearly two hours to get the herd contained and moved safely. By then, the deputies I'd learned Kaleb radioed for had swept the area but found no sign of the shooter. Just more shell casings matching the others, and fresh tire tracks leading to the county road.

When we finally dismounted, Cici's hands were shaking. I caught her arm as she stumbled, pulling her against me before I could think better of it. She didn't move away. Her heart was racing against my chest, and I found myself wanting to promise her everything would be okay. But we both knew better than to believe it would.

"Are you hurt?" I asked, my voice rougher than intended.

She shook her head against my chest. "Porter, if you hadn't been here…"

"But I was." I forced myself to step back, to remember all the reasons she and I couldn't be together again. At least not yet. The secrets I carried about Maverick, about the trust requirements, about my growing suspicions regarding her parents' death—they formed a wall between us that felt insurmountable. "And I'm not going anywhere. Not until we figure out who's behind this."

She studied me for a long moment, her eyes searching mine for something I wasn't sure I could give. "Why? Why risk yourself for us?"

Because I promised your father. Because I owe your brother. Because watching you fight so hard makes me want to fight beside you. Because every time I look at you, I forget all the reasons I shouldn't. Because I fucking love you, Cici Morris.

"Because it's the right thing to do," I said instead.

"Wait, Stormchaser?" she shielded her eyes from the sun and looked around.

"I got her into the barn, ma'am," said Stetson, who was standing a few feet from us. "She stumbled, but everything below the knee looks fine."

"Cici, this is Stetson Hamilton. He's—"

She nodded. "I know who he is. Thank you for taking care of Chaser."

Stet touched the brim of his hat with one finger. "I'm here to help, ma'am."

"My name is Cici. Use it," she said before turning to me. "We should check those shell casings again. Maybe there's something we missed."

"Once things have settled, I'll introduce you to the rest of the crew who came over from the Roaring Fork."

"You'll do more than that, Wheaton," she snapped without looking at me.

I followed her back to where the shots had come from. A spent casing glinted in the dirt, partially hidden under a scrub oak. Something about it caught my eye.

"Custom loads," I said, picking it up. "Not something you'd find at the local gun shop."

Cici crouched beside me. "These casings—" She stopped talking, and the color left her face.

"What is it?"

"Nothing." But her voice shook slightly. "Just remembered something I need to check in Dad's files."

Before I could press her, Johnson called from the fence line. Several posts had been damaged in the stampede, leaving a section unstable. If we didn't fix it before dark, we might lose the whole herd.

Every one of us worked side by side for the next few hours, setting posts and stringing wire. The physical labor helped quiet my mind, but I couldn't get over thinking that Cici had realized something important. Something that scared her.

Thunder Cloud grazed nearby, keeping watch like he sensed the lingering danger. The stallion had proved himself again today—steady under pressure, quick to respond. Just like his owner had been before everything went wrong.

"Your father would be proud," I said quietly as we finished the last section. "Of you, the way you're fighting for this place."

"Would he?" Her laugh was bitter. "Everything's falling apart, Porter. The breeding program, the contracts, the ranch itself. And now, someone's trying to kill us."

"They're trying to break you." I grabbed her arm as she started to turn away. "Don't let them."

She looked down at my hand gripping her sleeve, then back up at me. Something shifted in her expression—not quite trust, but maybe understanding. "Is that what you're doing? Refusing to break?"

The question hit closer to home than she could know. Every day I stayed sober was a victory over the guilt and secrets threatening to drown me. Every time

I chose to keep Maverick's secret, I broke a little more of whatever was growing between Cici and me.

"We should head back," I said instead of answering. "Storm's coming."

Dark clouds were gathering over the mountains, promising more complications.

"The herd needs to be checked for injury," I shouted in Thorn's direction. "We also need to make sure water access is secure."

"On it, boss."

"Who's that?" she asked on our way to the barn.

"Thorn Roseman, err, first name's Nash. He's assistant ranch foreman at Roaring Fork. You know him?" I asked when I noticed her scrunched eyes.

"Don't think so. I mean, I doubt I'd forget someone that good-looking."

My brow furrowed as I studied her, trying to figure out if she was giving me shit. However, it wasn't the first time I'd heard such comments about the guy.

Cici stopped walking and folded her arms. "You promised not to make major changes without consulting me first. And that you'd tell me everything—every problem, every solution, every detail."

"I know, and I'm sorry—"

"Wasn't it you who, only a few hours ago, said we need to start being honest with each other?"

"Yes."

"What else haven't you told me?"

I turned toward the barn, making it appear I was leading Thunder Cloud inside rather than refusing to look into her eyes. Where in the hell would I start if I came clean with all I hadn't told her?

Thunder Cloud's stride hitched slightly, making me realize he'd gotten nicked during the chaos. Nothing serious, but it was one more reminder of how close we'd come to disaster.

Cici must've picked up on it too since she didn't repeat her question. Once in the barn, she tended to Stormchaser while I led the stallion to his stall.

"How's she look?" I asked over my shoulder.

"Minor scrapes. Nothing serious." Still, I noticed Cici's hands tremble as she applied antiseptic.

"Let me help with Thunder Cloud," she said when she finished. "It's the least I can do after today."

I wanted to refuse her help, to say I could handle it, but the stallion had already moved toward her, nickering softly. Like father, like daughter—they both had a way with horses that went beyond simple training. Me, it was harder. For them, it came naturally.

She reached out, then pulled her hand back when she touched my arm and I flinched. "How are your burns healing?"

The truth was, I'd practically forgotten about them with everything else going on until her hand landed on one. "I'm fine."

"Sure you are." She smirked but didn't say anything else.

We worked in companionable silence, cleaning Thunder Cloud's small wound and checking him for other injuries. The barn was quiet except for the horses' soft movements and the distant rumble of thunder. Then Maverick's voice carried from outside, slurred and angry.

"Where is everyone? Cici?"

She tensed beside me, her hand stilling on Thunder Cloud's flank. "He's drunk again."

"I'll go," I said quickly. "We're pretty much done here."

"Porter—" She caught my arm, but in a different place, so this time, I didn't flinch. "Thank you. For today. For everything."

The gratitude in her voice made my chest ache with guilt. She was right to ask what else I hadn't told her, but that didn't mean I'd be able to answer.

Her hand lingered on my arm, and when our eyes met, God, how I longed to kiss her. Mav stumbling on the other side of the barn brought me back to my senses, and I hurried over to look for him.

I found him just inside the front alley door, an almost-empty bottle dangling from his fingers.

"Need a hand?" I asked, noticing he didn't have his crutches or his cane.

He squinted at me through the gathering darkness. "Heard there was trouble. Shots fired." His words slurred together. "Couldn't even help. Useless now."

"Let's get you inside before this storm hits," I said, doing my best to keep my voice steady.

"Why?" His tone was tinged with bitterness. "Why do you even care?"

Because watching you destroy yourself with alcohol reminds me of my own battles with the bottle.

"Because someone should," I said instead.

We'd gotten a few feet from the barn when lightning flashed, illuminating his face. For a moment, he looked so much like Hank it hurt. Then his legs buckled.

I caught him before he could fall, supporting his weight as the first fat drops of rain began to fall. "Come on, kid. Let's get you home."

"Everything's so messed up," he mumbled as I helped him toward the house. "Since the accident… since Mom and Dad…"

My heart clenched at the pain in his voice. We were almost to the ranch house when Cici raced up to us. "Maverick! Where are your crutches?"

"I got him," I said, helping him inside when she got the door open just as the storm broke in earnest.

I managed to carry him up to his room, then stood in the hallway afterward, listening to Cici's muffled words as she got him settled. The weight of our combined secret pressed down harder than ever. Maverick was spiraling, using alcohol to numb his demons. And Cici had recognized something about those shell casings that frightened her.

The truth was out there, hidden in the layers of lies and half-truths we'd all built around ourselves. I just hoped, when it finally came out, there'd be something left worth saving.

Thunder crashed overhead as I headed back to the barn to check Thunder Cloud and Stormchaser once more.

"What do you say, boy?" I murmured as I stroked the powerful horse. "Think your owner would forgive me if she knew the truth?"

The stallion nickered softly, offering no answers to questions that grew more complicated with each passing day.

"Hey," Cici said from behind me. "Are you coming back to the house?"

God, had she heard me? If so, she wasn't letting on. "Thought I'd call it a night."

"I meant it when I said I'd rather you stay there."

"I don't want to put—"

"Please, Porter. Do you have any idea how hard it is for me to ask?"

When she stepped closer and I saw she was crying, I pulled her into my arms. Her tears dampened the flannel of my shirt. "Shh," I soothed, reaching up to stroke her hair.

"I don't know how much more I can take."

I leaned away enough to see her face. "That's what they're counting on. We aren't gonna let them win. Do you hear me?"

Her eyes darted back and forth between mine. "I wish I knew why you cared so much."

I shook my head. "I always have."

"I thought you'd stopped."

"Never."

The way our lips met, I couldn't say which of us had instigated the kiss. All I knew was I wouldn't be the one to end it.

10

Cici

The custom shell casings I'd pulled out sat on Dad's desk like accusing fingers. Until now, I hadn't realized that each one represented a threat, a warning, a promise of violence. But it wasn't just their presence that made my hands shake—it was realizing the ranch had been in the same amount of danger before my parents died as it was now.

I ran my palm over Dad's worn leather desk chair, remembering how he used to sit here late into the night, going over financial reports and making calls to his network of contacts. The room still smelled like him—leather and the hint of aftershave he'd worn since before I was born. The scent made my throat tight with memories.

"What spooked you earlier?" Porter's voice was gentle but insistent. He'd been watching me since we returned to the house. Before that, actually. He'd noticed my reaction at the fence line, those perceptive eyes missing nothing. The way he leaned against my father's desk reminded me so much of how Dad used to stand there that it was hard to breathe.

I picked up one of the casings, turning it over in my palm. "I found these a while back but didn't think they were significant. Not until today." I set them in front of Porter. "These are match-grade ammunition. Custom loads, like you said. My dad used to special order them from a guy in Wyoming. Said they were the only rounds he trusted for long-range shooting."

Porter went still. "You're saying these came from your father's supplier?"

"The engravings match. See this stamp?" I pointed to a tiny mark near the rim. "Dad told me once it was like a signature. The guy who made them was proud of his work, wanted people to know where they came from."

"Do you remember his name?"

I shook my head. "Dad handled all that. But…" I pulled open the bottom drawer of his desk, rifling through old receipts and documents until I found what I was looking for. "Here. This is the last order he placed."

Porter studied the paper, his jaw tightening. "This was dated two months before the accident."

"Exactly." My voice cracked. "Which means either someone got access to Dad's supplier, or—"

"Someone knew your father's contacts." He set the receipt down.

The implications made me feel sick. Before I could respond, the sound of breaking glass echoed from the other room, followed by shouts of anger, which had us both racing in that direction.

Maverick had returned downstairs and was standing near the kitchen, whiskey bottle in hand, facing off with the sheriff. Shattered glass from a picture frame crunched under his feet.

"You don't get it," Mav was saying, his words slurring. "None of you understand what—" He stopped when he saw us, swaying slightly.

Something passed between Porter and Kaleb—a look loaded with meaning that made my skin prickle. They knew something. Something about my brother that they weren't sharing.

"Mav," I started, but he cut me off.

"Don't." He pointed the bottle at me accusingly. "Don't use that tone. Like you're so fucking perfect, so in control." His laugh was bitter, hollow. "At least I'm honest about being broken."

"That's enough." Porter's voice was quiet but firm.

"Or what?" Mav challenged. "You'll stop me like—" He caught himself, fear flashing across his face before the anger returned.

"Maverick." I stepped toward him, glass crunching under my boots too. "Please. Talk to me. What's really going on?"

For a moment, I saw my little brother again—scared, vulnerable, desperate for something he couldn't name. Then the walls slammed back up. He hurled the bottle to the floor and stumbled outside.

"I've got him," Porter said before I could move. He caught up to Mav, but they were too far away for me to hear what he was saying. Whatever it was made my brother's shoulders slump in defeat.

I watched in amazement as Porter guided him farther away from the house. As much as I wanted to follow, I could feel Kaleb's presence behind me.

"Do you know what's going on?" I asked.

He nodded. "It isn't my story to tell."

"Whose is it?"

"Porter's. And Mav's."

There was something in the way he phrased it. "Are they different?"

"You'll have to ask them. I got a call I need to follow up on. If you need me to come back later, just let me know."

I wasn't sure what that meant. Did he think we'd have another round of shots fired or animals hurt? I couldn't think about that now. I was too worried about my brother.

Twenty minutes later, Porter returned to the house with a much calmer Maverick. How had he done that? How had he reached my brother when I couldn't?

After getting Mav settled in his room, Porter found me in the kitchen, staring into a cup of coffee that had long gone cold.

"How did you get through to him?" I asked without looking up.

He was quiet for so long I thought he might not answer. Finally, he pulled out a chair and sat across from me. "Because I know what it's like. The guilt, the anger, the need to numb it all." He took a deep breath. "I've been pretty much sober since before Christmas."

Christmas? That made no sense. The accident happened between then and now. The one where Mav had almost lost his life.

A crash from outside interrupted whatever accusation I was about to hurl at him. We both jumped up, but it was just a branch hitting the window. The storm that had been threatening all evening finally arrived.

"Come sit with me," he said, leading me into the living room, where we both settled on the couch.

As we listened to the wind and snow swirling outside, Porter told me about his own battles with alcohol, about hitting rock bottom, about choosing sobriety one day at a time.

I found myself sharing too—about the pressure of trying to keep the ranch afloat, about watching Mav spiral, about missing our parents so much it physically hurt.

I didn't bring up the fact that he'd been drunk the night his truck hit Mav's. It felt wrong. He must've slipped up, had a drink that night, and when one led to several more, he'd gotten behind the wheel of his truck and almost killed my brother. Those had to be demons he was dealing with now, doing his damnedest to get his sobriety back under control. Regardless of what I said, it wouldn't change what happened, so I let it be.

Somewhere between the stories we shared, my head found his shoulder. His warmth and the steady sound of his breathing lulled me into a peace I hadn't felt in months. The last thing I remembered was his hand stroking my hair, his voice a low rumble as he talked about his first horse.

I woke briefly when he lifted me, strong arms cradling me against his chest as he carried me upstairs. Part of me wanted to protest that I could walk, but a larger part savored the feeling of being taken care of. It had been so long since I had someone do that.

"Stay," I murmured as he pulled the covers back, set me on the bed, then tucked me in. Yeah, I was still wearing the same jeans and flannel shirt I'd had on all day, but as tired as I was, I didn't care.

His hand brushed my cheek with a featherlight touch. "Get some sleep, Cici." I felt the mattress dip when he sat on the opposite side—on top of the covers rather than under.

As I drifted off again, I thought about the timeline he'd revealed. About that look between him and Kaleb. About all the little things that didn't quite add up about the second accident that shook my already devastated world after the loss of our parents.

But for tonight, I let myself believe in the safety of his presence, in the possibility that not everyone who came into our lives was meant to destroy them. That maybe—just maybe—things would work out between him and me this time. When I rolled toward him, he drew me closer so my head rested on his chest, and I wrapped my arm around his waist. God, I missed the feel of him in bed, beside me.

Tomorrow would bring new threats, new questions, new reasons to doubt. But right now, in the quiet dark of a stormy night, I allowed myself to trust in the strength of Porter Wheaton and the mysteries of his heart.

11

Porter

When I woke and Cici was still asleep, I got out of bed and stood by the window, watching the sunrise paint Morris Ranch in colors only seen in Colorado. Without looking over my shoulder at her for fear I'd crawl in beside her and not leave until I'd made her mine again, I thought about how good she'd felt in my arms. Her trust in me made my chest ache with equal parts longing and guilt. She believed I was here to help, and I was—but not for the reasons she thought.

My phone felt heavy in my hand as I stepped out of the room, went downstairs, and scrolled until I found Decker Ashford's number. He answered on the second ring despite the early hour.

"Porter Wheaton. Been a while."

"Too long. Listen, Deck, I'm calling because I need your help." I outlined the situation at Morris Ranch, keeping the details vague but emphasizing the urgency. "We need a full security upgrade. Yesterday."

"Shots fired, mysterious accidents, and arson attempts?" His voice sharpened with interest. "Sounds personal."

"That's what I'm afraid of. How fast can you get a team out here?"

"I'll head out in a couple of hours." He paused. "But, Porter, if this is as serious as it sounds, you might need more than just cameras and sensors."

"I know it." I rubbed the back of my neck.

"I'll bring backup. I've got a couple of guys who can stay on after I leave."

I thanked him, then called Buck.

My brother answered with his usual gruff. "What?"

"Need a favor." I told him Decker was on his way, and with some of the repairs we needed to make, I figured he'd spot any weaknesses I might have missed. "This place needs help, Buck. Real help."

He was quiet for a moment. "Give me a couple of hours to wrap up here. I'll bring some guys who worked on the system Decker set up here. Less of a learning curve. Oh and, Port, when I get there, you can tell me the rest of whatever it is you're leaving out."

"Thanks." I hesitated. "Have you, uh, heard from Holt?"

"He's between tours. Want me to have him come along?"

"Yeah. We could use all the hands we can get."

The next call was harder, but Cord had sent enough messages that I owed it to him to respond. He picked up immediately, like he'd been waiting.

"How are you, Port?"

Hearing his voice, the brother I was closest to, opened the dam of my emotions. "Not good, man. Someone's trying to destroy Morris Ranch." I lowered my voice and looked over my shoulder, making sure neither Cici nor Maverick were within earshot. "I think they killed Hank and Lillian to do it."

The silence on the other end stretched. "You sure about that?"

"No, but too many things don't add up." I told him about the shell casings, the sabotage, the escalating threats.

"Fuck," I heard him mutter in the background. "I wish I could be there, Port."

"I appreciate it, brother, but if anyone gets why you can't be, it's me. Buck too."

"I gotta say that even with all this shit you're telling me, you still sound better than I've heard you in a damn long time. Are you and Cici—"

"No," I snapped too quickly.

"But you're getting there."

"What are you? Clairvoyant?"

He chuckled. "Nope, but I am a man in love, so I recognize the signs."

"I've loved her for a long time, Cord."

"I know, Port."

"There are things I can't—" I stopped talking when I heard her footsteps on the stairs. "I gotta run. We'll talk more later."

I turned around to face her, nearly gasping when the sight of her made my heart stutter. Fuck, if she didn't make me want to carry her right back up those stairs and spend the day getting to know her naked body the way I used to.

"Good morning," she said, her cheeks flushing as though she could read my mind. "Do I smell coffee?"

I chuckled. "Not yet, darlin'. I had some calls to make."

"Dang it," she said, walking toward the kitchen, but not without looking over her shoulder and winking. "So, you said calls?" She asked after handing me a steaming mug.

"Yeah." I took a sip, buying time. "Got some more help coming. People I trust."

Her eyebrows rose. "You sure that's wise? Bringing in outsiders?"

"These aren't outsiders. They're family—Buck and Holt." I set down my coffee when her brow furrowed. I knew it had nothing to do with my brothers. She knew them both, and they'd always gotten along. "Cici, the ranch is vulnerable, and there's a lot of work that needs to get done in a hurry."

She started to protest, then stopped, her expression shifting. "You're right." She moved to the window, staring out at the land her father had built into something special. "I've been trying to do everything myself for so long that I forgot what it was like to have help I could count on."

The same trust I'd felt last night echoed in her voice, cutting deep. I set the cup down that I'd just picked up again and placed my hands on her shoulders. "I meant what I said about not letting them win."

She turned in my arms, her face tilted up to mine. "I know you did." Her fingers traced my jaw. "I just wish…"

"What?"

She shook her head.

"Come on, tell me. You just wish what?"

"I could be sure this is real."

She meant between her and me, and as much as she needed my reassurance, I couldn't give it to her. There were too many other things at play here. Things that, once she learned the truth, she might never forgive me for.

"I'm here, Cici. Believe in that."

"I want to…"

The sound of breaking glass from the other room shattered the moment. We both knew what it meant— Maverick was awake and probably already drinking, if not still drunk.

Cici pulled away, conflict clear on her face, but I wrapped my arm around her waist.

"Let me," I said. "I need to head into town anyway. I'm meeting Kaleb." And my AA group, but I didn't say that part, even though I had every intention of inviting her brother to come with me.

"You don't have to take on Mav, Porter. I understand you feel responsible, but his drinking started before, um, the accident."

I knew it had, far better than she'd ever know. "Let me do this, okay?"

She leaned up, kissed my cheek, and I watched her walk up the stairs instead of into the room where we'd heard her brother.

"Come with me," I said when I found him leaning against the counter, then walked out and hoped he followed. Since he was on crutches, I couldn't very well drag him like I wanted to.

"Where are we going?" he asked after climbing into the passenger seat of my truck.

"There are some people I want you to meet."

The AA meeting was already in progress when we slipped in. Kaleb nodded from his usual spot, eyes widening when he looked behind me and saw Mav. Rather than disrupt the person speaking more than I already had, I motioned to two seats in the back. After Maverick sat down, I took the seat beside him.

We listened as the man at the front of the room talked about making amends, about how sometimes the hardest person to forgive was yourself.

I'd taken a huge damn risk, bringing Mav in here, and I sure as hell hoped I didn't live to regret it. However, instead of storming out, he sat quietly, head hung, a tear rolling down his cheek.

I thought about some of the last words his father had said to me. "Sometimes, protecting people means making hard choices, son. Remember that." At the time, I was sure he was alluding to me breaking up with his daughter. And he would've been right that I'd done it to protect her.

Being at the ranch, sitting on the ticking time bomb of secrets I kept from her now, bringing Mav here with me, every single choice I was making was hard as hell. I just prayed they were the right ones.

After the meeting ended and we walked outside, Mav went straight to the truck and leaned against it until I unlocked it so he could get in while I waited for Kaleb.

"Hey," he said, glancing around me.

"Mav's waiting in the truck."

"Did he come of his own free will?"

I shrugged. "As far as the town at least. Gotta admit I didn't expect him to stick around."

Kaleb nodded. "On another subject, I feel as though we're missing something obvious with the shit happening at Morris Ranch. Something that's right in front of us."

"I agree. I mean, why that place specifically? There are other ranches for sale in the valley." I ran a hand through my hair. "Either way, there are easier ways to force a sale if that's what the person doing this is after." I didn't think it was, but I had no idea what else it could be.

"This feels different."

"Like someone's enjoying watching Cici and Mav suffer," I added.

"You think it's about revenge?"

"Nothing else makes sense."

Kaleb put his hand on my shoulder. "How are you doing?"

"One day at a time, my friend."

Back at the ranch, I found Cici in the barn with Thunder Cloud. The stallion nickered at my approach, and she turned, her eyes searching my face.

"How's Maverick?" she asked softly.

"Better. For now." Neither he nor I spoke on the ride home, which I hoped meant he was processing his feelings about the meeting.

She looked over at the house. "Is he inside?"

"Yeah."

"Porter?" She stepped closer. "Whatever's coming, whatever you're not telling me, just promise me one thing."

"Anything." The word came too quickly, and I regretted it.

"Promise you won't disappear. Not like you did before. Promise me that, if you have to leave, you'll tell me."

She was right about how I'd just vanished. I'd walked out of her life, wanting to hide my dependency on alcohol, one I hadn't been ready to admit even to myself. The excuse I'd told myself then was that we were too young, not ready for something so serious. Cici was nineteen at the time, and I was twenty-three, except she hadn't been the one too young to handle it; that was all on me.

I pulled her into my arms, knowing I might regret it as much as I did my last word. "I'm not going anywhere, Cici."

Not until the ranch was safe. Not until I'd kept my promise to her father. Not until I'd protected her brother's secret, even if it cost me any chance at a future with her. Not until so many other things, like discovering the truth about her parents' accident.

The wind picked up, carrying the scent of snow. Another storm was headed our way, another test of our resolve.

"Porter, I—"

"Shh," I said, kissing her before she could say more. If Cici Morris said the words I feared she was about to and I said them back, I'd never be able to keep my promise to her brother.

12

Cici

I came down the stairs after checking on Mav, who was sound asleep, but didn't see Porter in the living room, where he'd been a few minutes ago.

"Where did you go?" I said, going from room to room, looking for him. I finally found him in my father's office, with his phone pressed to his ear as he paced. The sight of him looking so at home in that space was like an unexpected blanket of warmth.

"No, sir, I understand," he said. "But if you could just confirm whether anyone else has ordered those specific casings from you besides Hank Morris." He paused. "Yes, I know it's been years." Another pause. "Got it. I appreciate your time."

He hung up, running a hand through his hair.

"The bullet maker?" I asked from the doorway.

He turned, not appearing surprised to see me there. "Yeah. Says Hank was his only client in this area. Never sold to anyone else."

"That's impossible." I moved to the desk, picking up one of the shell casings. "These were shot recently. Dad's been gone for two years." My voice caught.

"I know," Porter said quietly. "But the guy swears he hasn't made a single round since your father's last order."

The implication hung heavy in the air between us. Either the bullet maker was lying, or someone had gotten access to Dad's ammunition supply. Someone who'd been on the ranch, who knew where he kept things.

"We need to check the gun safe," I said. "Dad always stored extra rounds there."

Porter nodded. "Lead the way."

The safe was hidden in the back of the bedroom closet he and my mom used to share, behind his old rodeo trophies. The combination was my mother's birthday—something that had always made him smile. "You kids and your mama are the only sure things in my life," he used to say.

When I opened it, my heart sank. The shelves were empty except for a single box of shells. But those weren't the custom loads—just regular ammunition from the local sporting goods store.

"Someone cleaned it out," Porter said, examining the dusty shelves that were clear where boxes obviously used to sit. "Recently too, from the look of it."

"How would they know where to find them? The only people who knew about this safe were family and—"

"Longtime ranch hands," he finished. "People your father trusted."

"Someone came into the house? Into their room?" I sank onto the edge of my parents' bed when the implications made me dizzy.

From downstairs came the sound of Maverick moving around in the kitchen, followed by the clash of bottles in the recycling bin. The noise was a stark reminder of how fractured our family had become, how much life had changed since we lost our parents.

"Should we try talking to some of them? The ones who were here when my dad was alive?"

Porter shook his head. "I don't want them to know we suspect anything yet. By the way, the guy I mentioned who could help with security upgrades is arriving today. His name is Decker Ashford—"

"I can't pay him—"

He cut me off like I had him, except rather than use words, he kissed me. "I told you cost wasn't an issue."

"But how?"

He stroked my cheek. "You let me worry about that. Oh, and he isn't coming alone. He's bringing some of his crew, who will stay on after he's gone. And as I said, Holt and Buck should be here this afternoon too. I'll also make sure you meet Thorn, Bullet, and the other guys today."

"Thorn?" Earlier, when Porter had said the name, it sounded familiar, but I couldn't place it.

"I'm surprised you've already forgotten someone that good-looking," he deadpanned.

"Oh, I haven't."

Porter put one hand around my waist and pulled my body flush with his. "I might know a thing or two that could erase your memory of him completely."

Promises, promises, I wanted to say. Except no matter how much my body craved his, we weren't ready for that. We might never be. I realized Porter had just said something that I missed. "Sorry. Can you repeat that?"

"I said Thorn and the rest of the guys are staying in the south bunkhouse."

"Right. Good." When I glanced over at the empty shelves of the gun safe, a chill ran up my spine as I remembered something my dad always used to say. "Trust your gut, little girl. But remember—sometimes the truth isn't what we think it is."

My gaze met his. "Porter?"

"Yeah?"

"I'm scared."

He tightened his arms around me. "I know you are, Cici, and I'm going to do everything I can to make it so you don't have to be anymore, starting with upgrading the ranch's security."

"Upgrading?" I said, leaning far enough away to see his face. "Don't you mean installing one that works?"

He smiled. "Yeah, well, I was trying to be nice."

"You're sure about the cost? I really can't afford—"

He silenced me with another kiss, one that made my toes curl. It deepened until we were both breathless. When we finally broke apart, the sound of a truck approaching drew our attention to the window. A dark SUV pulled up the drive, followed by a work truck.

"That would be Decker," Porter said, his hand still resting on my lower back. "Come on. You should meet him."

Outside, a tall man in work clothes was already directing three others to unload security equipment. He turned as we approached, offering a friendly smile that put me at ease.

"Cici Morris," he said, extending his hand. "Decker Ashford. Porter's told me what's been happening here. We'll have you set up by nightfall."

Before I could respond, two more trucks pulled in. Porter's oldest brother, Buck, got out and waited for their younger brother Holt to join him before approaching us.

"Good to see you again, Cici," said Buck, hugging me. "Sure wish it was under better circumstances."

After Porter thanked both his brothers for being there, Decker asked us to walk the property with him, pointing out vulnerabilities I hadn't even considered. "Your current cameras haven't worked properly in months," he said, examining a unit near the barn.

"They haven't?" I asked. While I hadn't seen footage of anyone on the property, I had checked the feed regularly.

"The wiring's been damaged," Decker responded. "Mostly from weather and age, but some have been tampered with."

"Hey, Thorn," Porter said when another man approached.

When Decker paused, the man introduced himself.

"Miss Morris?" he stepped forward and said in a deep voice. "I'm Nash Roseman. Most folks call me Thorn." He nodded at Porter. "Got those fence supplies you asked me to bring."

A commotion from the barn interrupted my thoughts. We all turned to see Maverick in the doorway, his face pale. "Cici! Mesa King is down!"

Porter and I raced inside, followed by Thorn. The horse, one of our newer acquisitions and a most promising bucking-bronc prospect, lay thrashing in his stall, foam flecking his lips. My heart stopped when I saw the empty feed bucket.

"Call the vet," Porter said to Thorn, already kneeling down to check the horse's gums. *"Now!"*

The next hours passed in a blur of activity. Dr. Hanley arrived quickly, confirming my suspicion—someone had poisoned the bronc. As he worked to save him, Decker's team began installing security cameras and sensors throughout the property.

"He'll pull through," the vet said later, after ensuring Mesa King was stable, although weak. "He'll need constant monitoring for the next twenty-four hours at least."

I felt sick. Who could be so cruel? "I'll stay with him," I said. "I just need a minute." I rushed out to my truck and grabbed the rifle I'd aimed at Porter the day he arrived. It seemed so long ago, but in reality had been less than a week.

When I returned, everyone's eyes opened wide, except Porter's and Mav's, which made me chuckle. The other thing neither did was caution me to be careful. Had they, they would've gotten a quick buttstroke with the barrel.

Dr. Hanley gave me a list of symptoms to be on the lookout for and said to call him immediately if I noticed any of them.

When night fell, Porter came in to check on me like he had more than once in the last few hours.

"As promised, Decker's team finished installation," he said.

"How is that possible with the size of this place?"

Porter chuckled. "I said the same thing when they worked on the Roaring Fork's. I guess if you know ranches, you figure it out."

I still had trouble accepting that he and his crew would do all that work for free. Most likely, Porter was covering the cost, which I wasn't sure he could afford either.

"My brothers haven't finished with some of the projects they were tackling, but said they'd be back in the morning. Oh, and Decker said two of the guys who came with him will be here for as long as necessary. I put them in the north bunkhouse."

I cringed. "Tell them they can stay in the house."

He shook his head. "It's another one of their projects."

This time, I groaned. "I don't have the money, and you know it."

Porter sat down beside me, reaching out to stroke Mesa King's neck. "How's he doing?"

"Good so far."

"Oh, and Steel will train you on how the security system works tomorrow."

"Train me?"

Porter smiled. "It's pretty high-tech."

"How is he?" asked Mav, walking up to the stall.

"He'll be fine," I told him, even though I wasn't absolutely certain of that myself. At least not whether he'd still be a good bucking horse.

"Can we talk?" he asked Porter. "Alone?" he added when I started to stand.

I wanted to protest, but something in both of their expressions stopped me.

They'd only been gone a few minutes when Thorn approached. "Need a break?" he asked.

"I'm good."

"You need to rest."

I bristled. I'd have a hard time accepting anyone saying that to me except Porter or my brother. Even then, I might not take it well. Besides, there was no way in hell I'd leave the horse until I was certain he was past danger.

"As I said, I'm good."

He looked to his right when we heard footsteps. "Hey, Buck. Just seein' if Miss Morris needed anything before I called it a night," he said, taking a step away from the stall.

"I brought coffee. Is there anything else you can think of you need right now?" Buck asked.

I shook my head. "No, thanks."

"Okay, if I step in?" he asked.

"Of course."

He handed me the cup, then sat on a second cot I hadn't noticed someone brought in. "So, how are you holding up?"

"I'm okay."

"What's goin' on with you and Port?"

I shook my head. "You always were a damn gossip."

"You're probably right about that." He chuckled, then grew more serious. "The two of you are good for each other."

"I'm not sure about that."

"I am."

"He's keeping secrets," I said under my breath, admitting my fear for the first time.

"Aren't we all?" He studied me. "Sometimes, secrets protect people we love. Sometimes, they destroy us. The trick is knowing which is which."

"He broke my heart."

Buck nodded. "I know he did, and while it was different, he broke ours too."

I nodded, praying he didn't do it again. To any of us.

13

Porter

"Can we talk?" Maverick asked as we walked away from the barn where Cici watched over Mesa King. "About the meeting."

I nodded, leading him toward the fence line, where we could speak privately. The kid's hands trembled as he gripped his cane, whether from withdrawal or emotion, I couldn't tell.

The setting sun cast long shadows across the snow-covered ground, reminding me of the days that had passed since I arrived at Morris Ranch. Each one felt like walking a tightrope between truth and lies.

"How did you do it?" he finally asked. "Get sober?"

"One day at a time." The familiar AA mantra felt hollow, given the secrets I carried. "Some days are harder than others."

"How long?"

"Since Christmas." The words slipped out before I could stop them.

Maverick's head snapped up. "Christmas? But the accident—" He stopped, confusion clear on his face. "What happened that night? What made you drink again?"

How could I explain that I hadn't been drinking that night at all? That the story he believed—the one I'd let him believe—was a lie meant to protect him from his own actions?

The weight of it was suffocating, but all I could do was pray I was doing the right thing by Maverick and that, if Cici ever discovered the truth, she'd understand why I'd more than lied about what had really happened. Not only had I broken the law, but I'd begged my closest friend to go along with it, knowing he'd lose his job if anyone figured it out.

The memory of that old night in January surfaced unbidden too often. I'd been seventeen days sober, sitting across from Kaleb at our usual booth in the back of Annie's Diner, both drinking coffee, not whiskey.

The sheriff of Gunnison County became my AA sponsor on Christmas Eve, when he pulled me over and gave me a choice—get sober or go to jail. That night, I'd chosen to walk the straight and narrow. He let me sleep it off on his couch, hauled my ass to a meeting the next day, and saved my life.

Almost one month later, Kaleb had just finished his shift, still in uniform, while I was coming from a late meeting with a potential investor for the Roaring Fork.

"You look better," he'd said, dumping sugar into his coffee.

I remembered nodding, feeling proud of myself, but more, hopeful about the future. The irony of those thoughts would haunt me later.

It was nearly midnight when I headed home, taking the back roads out of habit—the same roads I'd driven drunk so many times before getting sober. Only this time, I was clear-headed when the headlights appeared around the bend, swerving into my lane.

Everything had happened fast after that. The impact. The sound of metal crushing metal. The airbag deploying with enough force to knock me senseless for a few seconds. When my vision cleared, I could smell gasoline.

My training kicked in—check yourself first. Nothing broken. Blood from a cut on my forehead, but my neck and back felt okay. I forced my door open and stumbled out, already reaching for my phone. Then I saw the other truck.

It had taken the worst of the impact, the front end crumpling like paper. The engine was still running, fuel was definitely leaking, and I could see someone slumped over the wheel.

Time slowed down as I made my way to the driver's side. The door was jammed, but the window had shattered. That's when I saw his face—just a kid, blood streaming from a gash on his forehead, and his leg bent at an angle that turned my stomach.

When the engine started making a sound I didn't like. I had to choose—try to kill it, or get the kid out first. The decision made itself when I saw flames licking under the hood.

"Hey! Can you hear me?" I reached through the window, checking his pulse. Strong, but his breathing was shallow. "I'm going to get you out of here."

It wasn't easy. The angle was bad, and I had to be careful of his leg. But adrenaline is a hell of a thing. I managed to pull him through the window and drag him away from the truck, putting as much distance between us and the leaking fuel as I could.

We made it about fifty yards before my legs gave out. I lowered him to the ground just as his truck's engine fully engulfed in flames. Holding him against my chest to keep him off the cold ground, I made two calls—first to Kaleb's personal cell, then 9-1-1.

That's when the kid stirred and I got my first real look at his face. My blood went cold as I recognized Maverick Morris. I'd just seen him last week, at the ranch, practicing for the state high-school finals. The kid was a natural on a bull, already making a name for himself at seventeen.

His eyes fluttered open, glazed and unfocused. That's when I smelled it—whiskey on his breath. The same poison that had nearly killed me so many times in my life.

"Don't…" he mumbled, trying to focus on my face. "Don't tell Cici…was drinking…she can't know…"

He passed out again, but the damage was done. I knew what a DUI would do to him. To the ranch. They were already struggling after losing their parents two years ago, and the legal fees alone would bankrupt them. Not to mention his bull-riding career—no sponsor would touch him with a drunk-driving conviction.

I heard sirens in the distance just as Kaleb's truck skidded to a stop nearby. He took in the scene, his face grim.

"Porter—"

"Take my blood." The words came out before I had fully formed the plan. "Take it now, before the ambulance gets here."

He stared at me. "What are you saying?"

"Switch the samples." I met his eyes, willing him to understand. "Make it look like I was drunk. I caused this. Not him."

"Are you insane? That's—"

"He's seventeen, Kaleb. His parents are dead. All he's got is his sister. You really want to be the one to destroy what's left of his life?"

The sirens were getting closer. Kaleb's jaw worked as he struggled with the decision. As both a sheriff and an EMT, he was uniquely qualified to make the switch.

"Please." I tightened my hold on the unconscious kid. "I can take the hit. I've been there before. But him? This will destroy everything—the ranch, his career, his relationship with his sister. Cici's already lost too much."

Maverick stirred again, moaning in pain. His leg was definitely broken, probably in multiple places. In the distance, his truck burst into flames.

Kaleb cursed, then grabbed his medical kit from his vehicle. "This is wrong on so many levels."

"I know." I held out my arm. "Do it anyway."

The next few hours were a blur. The ambulance arriving. Maverick being rushed into surgery. Me being arrested, playing the part of the drunk driver perfectly. I had years of experience to draw from, after all.

The hardest part was Cici's face when she saw me at the hospital. The hatred in her eyes. I wanted to tell her the truth—that her brother had made a mistake, that I was trying to protect him. But I couldn't. Not without undoing everything that had already been set in motion.

Later, after I was released on bail, Kaleb told me Maverick had no memory of the accident. The doctors chalked it up to trauma and a severe concussion. Only three people knew the truth—me, Kaleb, and Maverick, though he might never remember it.

The weight of protecting that secret felt like carrying Morris Ranch itself.

"This secret dies with us," Kaleb said the next day, standing in his kitchen after I got out of jail. "No one can ever know. It would destroy all of us—you, me, the kid. His whole future."

I nodded, already feeling the heaviness of the lie settling onto my shoulders. "I know."

What I didn't know then was how that pressure would get heavier. How watching Cici struggle to keep the ranch afloat while hating me would tear at my soul. How seeing Maverick's dreams of bull-riding glory die anyway, given how bad his leg was injured, would haunt my nights.

But I'd make the same choice again. Because, sometimes, the truth does more harm than good. Sometimes, the only way to protect the people you care about was to let them hate you.

And sometimes, the hardest part wasn't keeping the secret—it was living with the consequences of your choice.

The decision I'd made in that moment to take the blame, to let everyone believe I was the drunk driver, seemed simple then. Now, it was a chain around my neck, growing heavier with each passing day.

"Porter? Did you say you've been sober since Christmas?"

Before I could respond with yet another lie, my phone buzzed, offering me an escape. "Sorry, I need to take this."

The caller ID showed RodeoHouston.

"Mr. Wheaton, this is Tommy Wilson from the rodeo board," he said when I picked up. "I'm calling about the Morris Ranch contract."

"What about it?"

"We've received evidence that their stock program is compromised. I'm afraid we can't honor the agreement."

"What evidence?" My voice came out sharp, drawing Maverick's attention.

"I'm not at liberty to discuss the details, but the decision is final."

The line went dead before I could protest. Fury rose from deep in my chest—someone was systematically destroying every chance the ranch had at recovery. First, the equipment sabotage, then the fire, now this. The pattern was too deliberate to be a coincidence.

"Bad news?" Maverick asked, his earlier questions about sobriety momentarily forgotten.

"We're out in Houston." I didn't elaborate, but I could see him processing what this meant for the ranch.

"Because of me?" His voice cracked. "Because of what happened that night?"

"No. Absolutely not," I said firmly. "Someone's feeding them false information about the stock program. We'll fight it. I don't know what kind of proof they have, but whatever it is has been fabricated."

"I'm fucking cursed," he mumbled, gripping his cane tighter.

"This has nothing to do with you, Mav."

"You'll never understand," he said, hobbling toward the house.

I understood more than he'd ever know. The weight of secrets, the way guilt could consume you from the inside out—those were demons I knew intimately. There'd been plenty of times in my life when I believed I was cursed by being the *real* firstborn of Roscoe Wheaton.

How many times had I questioned whether taking the blame had really protected Mav or just delayed the inevitable? If he ever remembered what had really happened that night, would it destroy him? And what about Cici? What would it do to her?

"How did it go with Mav?" Cici asked when I returned to the barn.

I held up one finger when my phone buzzed again. This time, it was Decker, saying he needed to head out but would leave Steel and Jagger—both former CIA operatives—behind.

"The cameras are all operational," Decker reported. "But, Porter, there's something else you should know. The little footage we recovered from the old system before it was damaged had gaps. Specific gaps that coincided with the incidents."

"Someone with access and knowledge."

"Exactly. Be very careful who you trust."

"Understood," I said, ending the call after thanking him.

Who in the hell was the traitor in our midst, I asked myself again and again.

"What's going on, Porter?" Cici asked.

"The Houston contract fell through."

Her eyes scrunched. "Do you think it's connected to everything else?"

"Their board says they have evidence the program has been compromised."

Cici had been a part of the rodeo world, first as a competitor, then as a stock contractor for long enough to know exactly what that meant—one of their animals had tested positive for a banned substance.

When she bent her knees and lowered her head, I put my arm around her.

"I don't know how much more I can take, Porter. I mean it. It's all too much."

"You aren't alone anymore, Cici. I'm here. If you need to take a step back, do it."

She turned her head and looked at me. "What are you suggesting? That I go on vacation? Lay on the beach? Forget all the trouble here. Should I go alone? Leave Mav here—"

"Stop it. That isn't what I meant, and you know it."

She shook her head. "I don't. So how about you explain it to me?"

"What I mean is, lean on me as much as you need to. Yell, scream, pummel me with your fists. Take your anger, your frustration, everything you're feeling out on me."

Her eyes scrunched, and she was quiet so long that I thought maybe she'd let it go. I was wrong.

"Why, Porter? Why are you really here? Why are you taking all this on?"

"I told you already. I made a promise to—"

"My dad. But that isn't the only reason, is it? Did you think I wouldn't figure it out?"

Bile rose in my throat. "What are you talking about?"

"The real reason you're here."

"Why don't you enlighten me?"

Her eyes bored into mine. "Are you really going to make me say it?"

Thunder rumbled in the distance, promising another storm. Did she know I'd been forced to come here in order to save my family's legacy? Had she somehow found out what really happened the night of the accident? I reached into my pocket, touching the sobriety chip that got me through times like this.

"You know what? Fuck off, Porter. Fuck the hell off. I don't need or want your pity."

14

Cici

I stalked out of Mesa King's stall, not stopping until I'd walked all the way to the house, which was a *helluva* lot farther from the south barn than it was the north.

Once inside, I slammed the door as hard as I could. If I broke all the fucking windows in the house, I wouldn't give a shit. I couldn't do this anymore, and why the hell did I feel like I had to? The land alone had to be worth ten million bucks, maybe more. I could pay off all the debt and still wind up with enough money left over for Mav and me to be set for life.

Porter Wheaton could take his sorry ass back to Crested Butte and forget all about me. *Again.*

Did he really think I didn't know why he was here? That he felt so sorry for poor little Cici Morris, the girl whose heart he'd broken, that he promised her daddy to take care of her. Such a load of horse crap—something else I'd had enough of.

Whoever wanted us off this land was about to get their wish. I should've sold right after my parents' accident. Saved both my brother and me a ton of heartache. Maybe if I had, he never would've been in fucking Porter Wheaton's drunken path that night. His leg wouldn't be mangled, and he wouldn't be turning into an alcoholic at the age of seventeen.

As tempted as I was to pour myself a good stiff drink too, I didn't do it. Couldn't.

I looked out the window, knowing that no matter how angry I was at Porter or how many awful things I said to him, he wouldn't leave Mesa King's side. Sure, it meant I was relying on the man I said I didn't need or want, but he knew as well as I did that, no matter how many times I said it, it would never be true.

"Ceec?" I heard Mav say from upstairs. God in heaven, I could not deal with him tonight.

"Everything's fine. Go back to bed."

Did he listen? Of course not. Stupid kid. I spun around on him when he reached the bottom step, ready to light into him. Instead, when I looked him in the eye, I knew straightaway that he was sober.

"I guess you heard," he said, inching closer to me. "I'm sorry about Houston, sis." He held one arm out to me, and I fell into his embrace. God, how I needed this—Maverick not drunk and comforting me.

"I'm so tired," I said through my tears. "I can't do it anymore. I know I'm letting you down, but I just can't."

He leaned far enough away that he could look into my eyes. "You aren't letting me down. Don't think that. If you're done, I'm done."

"Porter will say we're letting them win."

Mav nudged me and grinned. "Who cares what he thinks?"

I did, and my brother knew it.

We both jumped when the door opened and Porter stalked in much in the same way I'd left the barn.

"What are you doing here?" I shrieked. "You left Mesa King alone?"

"No, I didn't leave him alone. He's got five people watching over him, one of whom is a vet."

"Oh my God. What happened?" I lunged for my coat and keys, then remembered I didn't have my truck.

"Nothing happened. Mesa King is fine, and if you don't believe me, get out your phone and look."

"What do you mean?"

Maverick nudged me again and held his phone where I could see it.

I gasped. "There's a camera in his stall?"

"There are cameras pretty much everywhere," Mav muttered.

My eyes widened as I looked between my brother and Porter. "Everywhere?"

"No, not everywhere. But yes, every inch of the barn is covered, as are all the outbuildings, equipment sheds, fence lines—"

"Got it," I said, cutting Porter off, taking Mav's phone from his hand, and walking over to the couch.

"Dr. Hanley came back to see how he was doing," Porter said, sitting next to me. "That was after I called in the cavalry, so to speak."

"I should go back."

"No, you should get some rest."

I looked over my shoulder at my brother, glad he'd said it before Porter could since, if he had, I'd already be on my way out.

"Hanley says Mesa King's recovery is going well. He also said that, while he isn't a medical doctor, he predicts that, if you don't get some rest, you'll end up in the hospital yourself."

As much as I didn't want to look into Porter's eyes, I couldn't stop myself. In them, I saw something that made me feel warm all over, but terrified me at the same time. I saw love.

"We need to talk," he leaned closer and whispered. "But not tonight."

I nodded, glad he didn't plan to force me to say the things out loud we both knew I was thinking.

"Mav, would you mind giving me some time alone with your sister?"

"Nope. I'm already on my way back to bed myself. Night, Ceec."

"Good night, Mav." I waited until I could hear the sound of him above us before speaking again. "He's sober."

"I know."

"Does this have something to do with your earlier conversation?" I asked.

"In part."

"Thank you."

Porter shook his head. "This is Maverick's journey."

"Still."

He stood and held his hand out.

"What?"

"Let's go to bed, Cici."

"I don't think that's a good idea."

"Then, I'll tuck you in and either find an empty bed down the hall or go back to the bunkhouse."

"I thought Decker's guys were sleeping there."

"First of all, Steel is with Mesa King and Jagger's on night duty, keeping an eye on this place. Second, there are more than two bunks. Now, either you get up and walk on your own, or I'll carry you."

"That isn't necessary—" Before I could finish my sentence, he scooped me into his arms. Rather than fight him, I rested my head on his shoulder. "I'm sorry I told you to fuck off."

"Not the first time I've heard it outa you. Probably won't be the last."

"Why are you being so nice to me after I was so mean to you?" I said when he set my body on the bed.

"You know why." He put his hands on either side of me and leaned closer. "And it isn't because I feel sorry for you." He stood up straight and turned to leave.

"Wait."

He stopped but didn't look at me. "What?"

"I don't want you to sleep in the bunkhouse."

"I think I remember seeing a couple more empty bedrooms up here."

"I don't want you to sleep in those either."

"What *do* you want, Cici?" he asked, finally facing me.

"Stay here with me."

He nodded once, walked around the end of the bed, and sat in the same place he had last night.

"I, um, need to use the bathroom."

"Don't worry, I'll still be here when you get back," Porter said, looking up at me when I stood.

In the days that followed, Porter and I formed a tentative truce, albeit one that did not include the same affectionate kisses we'd shared prior to the scene in the barn.

Mesa King's recovery became my world for the next two weeks. I was part of the rotation of those who slept in the barn with him, monitoring his vital signs, following Dr. Hanley's instructions to the letter. The stallion's strength returned slowly but steadily, each small improvement a victory against whoever had tried to kill him.

Each night I spent on a cot, Porter did too. And when I slept in my bed, he was there too.

Thorn and the rest of the guys proved invaluable during this time, handling whatever needed to be done without Porter or me having to ask. It seemed like everyone was anticipating issues before they arose—fixing fence sections that had to be repaired, helping with feeding schedules, stepping in wherever they saw a gap.

"Time for you to get some rest in a real bed," Porter said, appearing outside the stall after he'd returned from tackling some of the morning chores.

"I'm okay for a little while longer."

He shook his head. "We agreed whoever is with him at night takes the next day off."

The concern in his voice made my chest tight. I missed his touch so much, longed for it. At night, my body was drawn to his like a magnet. I'd drift over to his side of the bed, where he was covered by a blanket but remained above the sheets I was under. I'd sleep with my head on his chest. But, unlike the night before I told him to fuck off, his arm didn't naturally fall across my waist.

If he woke first, he'd ease out from under me and "escape" before I had the chance to say good morning. By the time I got downstairs, he'd be on his way out, usually with Maverick in tow.

While I was curious, something told me not to ask why they went to town as often as they did. That Mav hadn't been drunk for fifteen days—and yes, I was counting—hinted that their trips might have something to do with it.

"Mornin', Cici," said Thorn when I came into the barn for my daily check on the horse, whose recovery was progressing better than expected, at least according to the vet.

"Good morning," I responded, surprised to see Porter was there too. Was it my imagination, or did his gaze feel slightly warmer today? And was it only me who felt the air crackle when I stepped close enough that we could touch?

"I've got an errand to run," Porter said. "Wonderin' if you wanted to come with me."

I was about to ask why Mav wasn't going, but stopped myself. I'd seen so little of either of them. I'd take whatever time they were willing to give, alone or together.

"I'd like that," I said.

"I'll hold down the fort while you're gone," Thorn offered.

Porter nudged him. "Mighty nice of you, considering it's what you're being paid to do."

Both men chuckled.

Between him and the other guys from the Roaring Fork who showed up every morning and the two men who'd stayed when Decker Ashford left, there'd been no new incidents. The cameras covered every angle of the property.

Still, it was hard for me to shake the feeling that whoever was behind the attacks was simply biding their time.

"How's breakfast sound?" Porter asked once we were in his truck and driving out the ranch's gates. How long had it been since I ventured farther from the ranch house than the south barn?

"I'd love it. It feels good to get out."

"I should've thought of it sooner."

I turned to study him. His eyes were tight, like they'd so often been in the last two weeks. "Porter?"

He glanced in my direction. "What's up?"

"I want us to be okay—"

"We're fine," he answered too quickly.

It meant lowering my pride, but I had to go on. "You haven't kissed me."

His cheeks flushed, something I'd always found so sweet about the rugged cowboy. "I wasn't sure you wanted me to."

"Inviting you into my bed wasn't enough of a sign that I did?"

He stunned me by pulling off to the side of the road and parking. "You asked me not to leave. That's different."

"What if I didn't want it to be?"

Porter reached over and cupped my cheek. "You sure that's a good idea?"

I bristled as old insecurities landed like lead in my stomach. Was he letting me down easy?

"I asked you a question," he pressed.

"I won't beg, Porter."

His sexy smile nearly had me taking it back. "Tell me what you want."

"Kiss me."

Our lips met in a frenzy of bottled-up desire. His tongue probed deeply as his hand moved from my cheek to my neck. I'd always loved how assertive and demanding he was with the way he kissed, but more, when we had sex.

I groaned into his mouth at the memory of how good it had been between us. Better than good. Fantastic.

He pulled back and rested his forehead against mine. "Do you know how much I want you?"

"I don't."

"It's agony sleeping beside you every night—"

"You don't even touch me."

Porter kissed me again, just as passionately. "It's because I know if I do, I won't stop until we're both naked and I'm deep inside you."

I shuddered. "I want that."

He kissed me once more, then retreated to his side of the truck. "First, breakfast."

"If we have to," I said, winking.

15

I'd invited Cici to breakfast to talk about RodeoHouston's contract cancellation, and before I got sidetracked, thinking about how much I wanted us to be back at the house and in bed, I needed to give her an update.

I'd reached out to Matt Rice, who had connections on the board, but even he'd hit walls trying to uncover what prompted their decision.

"Someone sent them documentation," he'd told me over the phone yesterday. "Blood-test results, performance records—all indicating systematic doping of the stock."

"That's impossible," I'd growled. "Cici runs clean here."

"I know that. But whoever fabricated this evidence knew what they were doing."

"What do we do now?" Cici asked when I finished recounting the conversation.

"I'm going to talk to Buck. I don't feel comfortable asking Decker Ashford for more favors, but I've heard he's able to get information that no one else can."

"How?" she asked.

"I have a feeling it's better if we don't know." I pulled up and parked in front of Annie's Diner. "This all right with you?" I asked.

"Annie's is my favorite."

I remembered it was. I also knew she'd order the corned beef hash with a sunny-side-up egg and that, when I asked the waitress to bring out a cinnamon roll before the rest of our order, Cici would eat half of it, then ask if I wanted some, since I hadn't had a single bite. And that when I shook my head, she'd devour the rest. Then, she'd be too full to eat more than a quarter of her hash before offering it to me.

"I can't eat the rest," she said, true to form, after I'd polished off my own biscuits and gravy.

"You sure you don't want the leftovers?" I asked when she slid it in my direction.

"It doesn't taste the same," she said, also like she always had.

I wondered if she remembered our first time at Annie's. We were both kids at the time. Her by age, me by immaturity.

The memories of seeing her for the first time at the barrel-racing event at the Gunnison County Fairgrounds had sustained me in some of my darkest days. I stood at the fence that night, watching the riders warm up, and when I saw Cici come down the alley, my heart stopped.

Her long, dark hair was loose beneath the black felt hat she wore, and her pearl-snap shirt strained against her full breasts. Watching her move in her Cinch jeans had nearly been my undoing, especially when she sauntered past me in a captivating-as-fuck gait.

When she looked over her shoulder and her big brown eyes caught me looking, she'd smirked and gave a little toss of her head that had me wanting to follow her into the arena.

I later learned she was Hank Morris' daughter, was eighteen, fresh out of high school, and ranked in the top five of all barrel racers in the country.

Twenty-two at the time, I was making a name for myself in team roping. Kaleb had been the heeler to my header back then. I often wondered how far we could've gone if my drinking hadn't fucked things up for us.

Cici's eyes and mine met across the arena more than once that evening, and each time, something electric passed between us.

We kept running into each other at events after that. Each encounter charged with possibility until, finally, after a particularly high-scoring run around the barrels, I used an offer of congratulations to kiss her behind the stock pens. That kiss had led to more, to nights spent in my trailer or hers.

"You okay?" Cici's voice pulled me from the memory. Even from across the table, I could feel her heat and smell the familiar scent of her skin.

"Just remembering," I said.

"When we met?"

I shouldn't have been surprised she'd read my thoughts. Cici had always been pretty good, knowing what I was thinking. Good and bad.

"What about you?" I asked. "Do you think about it?"

Her eyes flared. "More than I should."

"I have to go to the Roaring Fork later," I said when a server I didn't recognize dropped off the check. "You want to ride along, or would you rather I drop you off at home first?"

"I definitely want to ride along. It feels so good to be off the ranch for a bit."

"Even if it's to go to another one?" I asked.

"I always loved the Roaring Fork. I can't remember the last time I was there."

"As I said earlier, I'm going to ask Buck if he can help us figure out what happened with RodeoHouston."

The drive to Crested Butte, where our family's ranch was located, felt longer than usual. I hadn't been back since the day I reported to Morris Ranch, and truthfully, I wasn't eager to return. Too many memories connected to the place, and most of them weren't good.

"It looks different," Cici said as we turned onto the familiar road. "The trees seem a lot bigger, and it looks, err, better run."

"That's mostly Buck's doing since he's the only one living here full time now." I didn't elaborate about why

Cord wasn't here. She already knew Holt was on tour most of the year.

Buck met us at the barn, his expression grim. "Got what you asked for," he said, leading us to the office.

He pulled out several documents, including lab reports from a testing facility I recognized as one of the most reputable in the industry. The paperwork showed elevated testosterone levels and other performance-enhancing substances in multiple Morris Ranch animals.

"These are fake," Cici blurted, studying one of the reports. "Look at the dates—they claim to have tested Thunder Cloud last month when he was recovering from the fire. But he never left the ranch."

"Good catch," said Buck. "But whoever created these knew enough about drug-testing protocols to make them look legitimate to someone who doesn't know better."

"The rodeo board wouldn't question reports from this lab," I added. "Their reputation is solid."

Cici's hands trembled as she set the papers down. "Someone went to a lot of trouble to make it look like we're doping our stock." Her head hung. "Just include it on the list of ways they're trying to fuck us over," she added under her breath.

"We'll fight this," I said. "Matt Rice might be able to help us prove these are forgeries."

"How?" she asked.

"The lab keeps detailed records of every test they run. If we can get them to confirm these reports didn't come from them…"

"It won't undo the damage to our reputation," Cici said quietly. "Even if we prove the documents are fake, other organizers will have heard the accusations and any protests on our part will go unheeded."

She was right. In the roughstock business, reputation was everything. Someone knew exactly how to hurt Morris Ranch where it would do the most damage in terms of getting the rodeo contracts we so desperately needed.

"One step at a time," I said, gathering the forged reports. "First, we prove these are fake. Then we figure out who created them."

"Hey, before you head out, there's something I need to show you," Buck said, motioning for me to follow him inside the main ranch house no one lived in anymore.

"Look, let's just talk about it and get it over with," he began. "You know what I'm talking about? Roscoe?"

"Cord told me you found out you're not his son."

What Buck had no inkling of was how long I'd known he wasn't—twenty-three fucking years. I was eight when Roscoe got drunk and dumped his fucking secret on me, making me swear on my mama's life that I'd never tell a soul. Even after she died, I didn't have the balls to do it.

"I just want you to know this doesn't change any-thing between us, Port. You're my brother, the same as you've always been. I love you, man."

God, I wanted to say those words back to him, but I couldn't bring myself to. Just like with Cici, once he found out the truth, that I could've spared him years of abuse at the hands of the old man, his mindset would change.

Buck waited for a few seconds, and when I didn't respond, he led me back outside.

"I'll be in touch if I find anything else out," he said. I didn't miss the way his eyes were hooded. I knew

I'd hurt him, but what could I say now? If I acted like everything was okay, it would just be another lie that he wouldn't be able to forgive me for when the truth finally came out.

The drive back to Morris Ranch was quiet, both Cici and I were lost in thought. I wanted to tell her everything would be okay with her family's ranch, but we both knew better than to make promises we couldn't keep.

Because the truth was, whoever had fabricated those test results knew exactly what they were doing. They understood how to make the forgeries convincing, knew which substances to list, even got the testing protocols right. This wasn't just about hurting the ranch's business. Once again, it was about destroying everything the Morris family had built.

I reached over and took Cici's hand, needing to feel her strength as much as offer my own.

"Listen, I said we needed to talk—"

"We don't have to," Cici interrupted.

"Yeah, we do. You need to know I've never felt sorry for you. Not once. Since the day I met you, you've been the strongest woman—person—I've ever known. Do I want to help you? Yes, I do. But not because I look at you as someone who can't help themselves. Everything that's happened at the ranch is more than most people could withstand, your dad included."

"That isn't true—"

"I'm not finished."

Her eyes opened wide, but she kept her mouth shut.

"I've never stopped caring about you. Even after…" I'd had no intention of bringing up the night I walked out of her life—now or ever. "Anyway, I haven't stopped. I'll care about you until the day I die."

We were through the Morris Ranch gates, and she still hadn't responded.

"Cici?"

"I heard you, Porter." She got out of the truck, and instead of walking in the direction of the house, she took off toward the south barn.

"Cici!" I shouted after her.

"Leave me alone, Porter."

I ran from the truck, not even bothering to shut the door. By the time I reached her, she was close to one of the storehouses. I grabbed her arm, pulled her to the opposite side of the building, and pushed her up against it.

"I'm not gonna leave you alone, Cicily Morris. Never again."

She raised her chin. "Why not?"

"You know why."

"Say it, Porter. Just fucking say it."

"Because I love you, goddammit." My mouth crashed into hers like I was a man dying and only her kiss could save me. And maybe I was.

16

Cici

Porter's mouth crashed into mine with a desperation that matched the words he'd just spoken. *I love you.* The declaration I'd longed to hear echoed in my head as his body pressed me against the storehouse wall. His kiss tasted of promises and possibility, of everything I'd been afraid to want since he showed up at the ranch. The rough wood caught at my jacket as he leaned into me, but I didn't care. All that mattered was the way his mouth moved against mine, hungry and demanding.

My hands found their way under his shirt, needing to feel his skin. The muscles of his stomach contracted at my touch, and he groaned into my mouth as his fingers tangled in my hair. God, how I'd missed this—missed him. The way he could make the world disappear with just a touch. The solid warmth of his chest under my palms reminded me of countless nights spent in his arms, back when I thought we'd be together forever. His heart hammered against my fingers, matching the wild rhythm of my own.

His familiar scent—leather and soap and something uniquely Porter—surrounded me as he deepened the kiss. I melted into him, forgetting everything else—the ranch's troubles, Maverick's struggles, the mounting threats. For now, all I cared about was being kissed breathless by a man I'd never stopped loving, no matter how hard I tried. My fingers traced the planes of his chest, remembering every scar, every mark, every inch of skin I used to know by heart.

His hands slid down my sides, gripping my hips and pulling me closer. The heat of his body seeped through my clothes, making me ache for more. I wanted to lose myself in this moment and pretend the last few years had never happened. That we were still those people who thought love could conquer anything.

The sound of breaking glass shattered the moment like a gunshot. Maverick's angry voice carried across the yard, slurred and thick with alcohol, yanking me back to reality with brutal force.

"Where is everyone?" he shouted. "Having fun without me?"

Porter's forehead rested against mine for a heartbeat, his breath coming in quick pants that matched my own. When we both turned toward the sound, my brother stood swaying on the porch, an empty bottle dangling from his fingers. Another lay shattered at his feet, shards of glass glinting in the late-afternoon sun. The sight of him there, drunk and angry, crushed the warmth of the earlier moments under a heavy blanket of guilt.

"This is my fault," I whispered, already moving toward the house. "We left him behind today." The words tasted bitter in my mouth, still swollen from Porter's kisses. Remorse crashed through me as I thought about how well he'd been doing lately, how his eyes had been clearer, his smile more genuine. All undone because I'd selfishly wanted time alone with Porter.

I remembered how happy Mav had seemed this morning, working with Mesa King despite the constant pain in his leg. He'd even joked with Thorn about something I couldn't hear, but his laughter had carried across the yard. Now, that progress lay shattered like the bottle at his feet.

"No." Porter caught my arm, his grip firm but gentle. "This isn't because of that."

No matter what he said, I wouldn't be able to stop feeling like I'd failed my brother again. He'd been going to town with Porter almost every day, and the one time we broke that routine, he fell back into the bottle. What kind of sister was I, getting lost in romantic moments while my brother suffered? Mom would have known what to do. Dad would have found the right words. But they were gone, and I was all Mav had left.

"Coming to check on me?" Mav's bitter laugh cut through the air like a knife. "Don't bother. I'm fine. Everything's just fucking fine." He kicked at the broken glass, nearly losing his balance. "You two looked cozy out there. Real sweet."

The mockery in his voice hurt worse than anger would have. This wasn't my brother—not really. This was pain and alcohol talking, twisting him into someone I barely recognized. The way he swayed made my heart clench.

He took a step forward and stumbled. Porter moved faster than I'd ever seen him, catching my brother before he fell into the broken glass. The move was practiced, like he'd done it before. How many times had he helped Mav when I wasn't around? The thought both comforted and troubled me.

"Let me go," Mav growled, trying to push him away. His words slurred together. "Don't need your help. Don't need anyone's help."

"Yes, you do." Porter's voice was firm but gentle, the same tone he used with spooked horses. "And that's okay. Everyone needs help sometimes."

Something in the way he said it made Mav stop fighting. His shoulders slumped as the anger seemed to drain out of him, replaced by defeat that broke my heart. This wasn't my wild, confident little brother who used to light up rodeo arenas with his smile. The boy who'd chased his dreams across eight seconds of fury on the back of a bull. This was someone lost, drowning in pain I didn't know how to help him escape.

I could smell the whiskey on him. The same bottles I kept finding hidden around the ranch. Each one felt like another failure on my part, another way I'd let him down.

"I saw you two," he mumbled as Porter helped him inside. "You don't have to hide it. Not from me. Not anymore."

"We weren't hiding anything," I said, following them up the stairs. Each step creaked under our weight, the sound as familiar as breathing. How many times had I helped him up these same stairs? How many more times would I have to? "We just—"

"Got caught up in the moment?" Mav's laugh was harsh, echoing in the narrow stairwell. "Yeah, I remember what that was like. Before…" He gestured at his leg, the movement uncoordinated and angry. "Before everything went to shit."

Porter's jaw tightened at Mav's words, but he kept his voice steady when he responded. "Let's get you to bed. You can sleep this off."

Once we got him settled in his room, I sat beside him on the bed that seemed too big for my little brother. My fingers found their way into his hair, stroking it like I used to when he was little and had nightmares. Back then, I could chase away his fears with a hug and a story. Now, I felt helpless against the demons that haunted him.

The dim light painted shadows across his face, making him look older than his seventeen years. How had we ended up here? When had I stopped being able to protect him?

"I'm sorry we left you behind today," I whispered, my throat tight with unshed tears. The words felt inadequate, like everything else I tried to do for him lately.

"Stop." He caught my wrist, his grip strong enough to hurt. "Not everything's your fault, Ceec." His eyes closed as the alcohol pulled him under, his voice growing softer. "Sometimes, things just are what they are."

I stayed until I was sure he was asleep, watching his face smooth out as consciousness faded. He looked like my little brother again—the one who used to crawl into my bed during thunderstorms, who'd beg me to watch "just one more" ride when he was practicing.

When I finally slipped out of his room, I found Porter waiting in the hallway, his expression unreadable. The passion from earlier felt like a distant dream, replaced by the harsh reality of our complicated lives.

"He's right, you know?" he said as we walked downstairs. Our footsteps echoed in the quiet house. "This isn't your fault."

"Then, whose is it?" I dropped onto the couch, suddenly exhausted. The weight of my confusing feelings for Porter pressed down on me until I could barely breathe. "I'm supposed to take care of him."

The words came out small and lost, like the little girl I sometimes still felt like, trying to fill shoes that were too big for me. The living room looked exactly as it had when our parents were alive—Mom's favorite throw still draped over the armchair, the book Dad was reading still on the bottom shelf of the end table. Sometimes, I felt like I was playing house in a museum of memories.

"You do take care of him." Porter sat beside me, close enough for me to feel his warmth. The cushions dipped under his weight, drawing us closer together. "But you're allowed to have a life too, Cici. To want things for yourself."

I turned to face him, needing to see his eyes. The lamp cast shadows across his face, highlighting the strong line of his jaw and the concern in his expression. "Are we going to talk about what you said?"

"Yeah." He reached for my hand, his thumb tracing patterns on my palm that sent shivers up my arm. The simple touch somehow felt more intimate than our earlier passionate kisses. "I meant it, Cici."

"But?"

"No buts." Yet something in his expression made me wonder. There was a hesitation there, a shadow behind his words that I couldn't read. It reminded me of the careful way he held himself apart from me at night, even as he let me use his chest as a pillow. Like there was an invisible line he wouldn't allow himself to cross.

"Porter…" I shifted closer, searching his face for answers to questions I wasn't sure how to ask. His scent wrapped around me like a familiar blanket. "If you're having second thoughts—"

He cut me off with a kiss, softer than the ones we'd shared outside but no less intense. His hand came up to cup my cheek, and his thumb stroked along my jaw-line. "The only thing I'm thinking about is how much I want this. Want you."

God, how I wanted to trust in his words, the heat of his kiss, the way his fingers felt as they trailed down my neck. But there was something in the way he touched me—like he was afraid I might break, or maybe afraid he would.

"What aren't you telling me?" I whispered against his lips, tasting the mint of a recent stick of gum.

When he pulled back, his eyes were scrunched, that familiar expression that meant he was wrestling with something inside himself. "Cici…"

"No, forget I asked." I pressed my fingers to his lips, stopping whatever half-truth he might have offered. "I don't want to push. Not tonight." Not when I was still reeling from the emotional whiplash of the past hour—from passion to fear to this uncertain place where hope and doubt tangled together in my chest.

"Stay with me again?" I asked instead, choosing the comfort of his presence over the uncertainty of his secrets.

He nodded, following me upstairs. Like every night for the past two weeks, he lay on top of the covers while I slid beneath them. The mattress dipped as we found our usual positions, my body gravitating toward his, my head finding its place on his chest. His heartbeat was steady under my ear, a rhythm I'd memorized in the nights we'd spent this way.

His arm draped around my waist, and I tried to focus on the comfort of his touch rather than the questions that swirled in my mind. Why did he maintain this careful distance even as he claimed to want me? What was he holding back? And why did his declaration of love feel both completely right and somehow terrifyingly tentative?

The cotton of his T-shirt was soft against my cheek, but I missed the feel of his skin. Missed the intimacy we used to share so easily.

"I can hear you thinking," he murmured into my hair.

"Just wondering how we got here," I said, not entirely lying. My fingers played with a loose thread on his shirt. "A month ago, I would have sworn I'd never let you back into my life."

His chest rose and fell with a deep breath. "Do you regret it?"

"No." The answer came instantly, surprising me with its certainty. Despite everything—the confusion, the doubts, the feeling that he was keeping something from me—I couldn't regret letting Porter Wheaton back into my heart. Maybe I'd never truly pushed him out, in the first place.

Sleep was a long time coming as I lay there, listening to him breathe. Outside, the wind picked up, rattling the windows with the promise of another storm. It felt fitting somehow—this wild weather matching the turbulence in my heart as I tried to reconcile the passion and love Porter offered with the sense that I couldn't trust it.

His arm tightened around me as a particularly strong gust shook the house, a protective gesture that made my heart ache. I wanted this—wanted him—so badly it hurt. But I couldn't stop thinking that whatever he was holding back had the power to shatter everything we were rebuilding.

Tomorrow would bring new challenges, new worries about Mav, new questions about who was trying to destroy our ranch. But for tonight, I let myself be held by the man I loved, trying to believe that, this time, love might be enough to overcome whatever secrets lay between us.

17

Porter

I woke to find Cici pressed against me, her head tucked under my chin, one leg thrown over mine. We'd fallen asleep in our usual positions—me on top of the covers, her underneath—but sometime in the night, she'd managed to wrap herself around me anyway. Her warmth seeped through the blanket between us, making my body ache with the need to pull her closer.

Last night's confession echoed in my head. Telling Cici I loved her was the truest thing I'd ever said to her, but it was still shadowed by lies. I gently extracted myself, not wanting to wake her. She made a small sound of protest that nearly broke my resolve, but I had somewhere to be.

Maverick waited downstairs, his face pale and drawn. No crutches today—a good sign. His determination to walk without them filled me with pride I didn't deserve to feel.

"Ready?" I asked, keeping my voice low, though we were far enough from the house that Cici wouldn't hear.

"I remembered something," he finally said as we turned onto the main road. "About that night. The accident."

My hands tightened on the steering wheel. "Mav—"

"Not all of it. Just…flashes. The sound of metal crushing metal. Someone pulling me out…" He stared straight ahead. "Your voice."

"Memory's tricky when trauma's involved," I offered. "The doctors said—"

"Stop." His voice cracked, and his eyes filled with tears. "Just…don't say anything else."

I pulled over, killing the engine. "What's goin' on, Maverick?"

"Why are you helping me?" he finally asked. "After everything…"

"Because it's the right thing to do."

"Is it? Look at me, Porter. Look at what I've become." He gestured at his leg. "A crippled drunk. Some fucking legacy."

"You're not—"

"I'm exactly what everyone thinks I am. Except they blame the wrong person for it." He reached for the door handle. "I can't do this anymore. I can't watch you and Cici…watch you try to fix everything while I just keep breaking it."

"Where are you going?"

"I don't deserve your help. Any of it." He got out, stumbling in the dirt. "Tell Cici…tell her whatever you want. You're good at that."

I got out too, rounding the front of the vehicle. "Get back in the truck."

"Or what? You'll take the blame for this too?" His laugh sounded more like a cackle. "Everything you touch turns to shit because of me. You think I don't notice? How you hold back, not just with me. More with Cici. I may not know exactly what, Porter, but I damn sure know you're walking a tightrope, and it's because of me."

"Nothing I'm doing is because of you, Mav."

"No? Then, why are you really helping out at the ranch? Why now?" He took a step back when I reached for him. "I'm not stupid. I see how you struggle to come up with answers to questions you'd rather not address. I see a fuck of a lot more than you think."

I shook my head. "Quit wasting time trying to figure me out. Focus on yourself—getting sober and getting the ranch back on track. Now, get in the truck. I don't want to miss the meeting. I need it, man."

When Maverick climbed in without further argument, I shut the door behind him.

But after I got in and glanced over at him, I saw he was crying in earnest.

"I'm sorry. For all of it. Mostly, I'm sorry for everything Cici has been forced to deal with. Until you showed up, she had no help at all. Especially not from me. I just made it all worse." He put his head in his hands, and his shoulders shook.

I started the engine and drove the rest of the way to town, thinking about Cici the entire time. When I'd left her, she was sleeping peacefully in the bed we shared but didn't. About the love I'd finally admitted but couldn't fully claim. About the web of lies and half-truths that threatened to strangle us all. My guilt and remorse were similar to Maverick's, except mine were a lot worse.

The AA meeting was hard. Mav sat in the back corner, arms crossed, radiating tension. He didn't speak, didn't even look up when others shared their stories. But he stayed. That was something. Each time he came, he appeared to be listening a little more. Today, I caught him nodding once when someone talked about using alcohol to dull memories they couldn't face. Baby steps. That's what Kaleb always said—recovery was about putting one foot in front of the other, regardless of how far you travel.

When we returned to the ranch, Cici was waiting on the porch. The sight of her there, wrapped in one of her dad's old cardigans against the morning chill, made my chest tight. She'd pulled her hair back in a messy bun, and her eyes were still heavy with sleep. Beautiful in a way that made me ache.

"Everything okay?" she asked as Mav headed inside without a word.

"Yeah." I climbed the steps, wanting nothing more than to pull her into my arms. "He's just processing some stuff."

She studied my face. "You look exhausted."

"Didn't sleep much."

"Me either." Her hand found mine, fingers intertwining. "I missed you this morning."

The simple touch sent warmth through my entire body. "I didn't want to wake you."

"I wouldn't have minded." She stepped closer, and I caught the scent of her shampoo—something floral and familiar that reminded me of better days. "Porter…"

"Cici." My free hand came up to cup her cheek. "About yesterday—"

"Don't." She pressed her fingers to my lips. "Don't take it back."

"I wasn't going to. I meant what I said. Every word."

Her eyes searched mine, and I wondered what she saw there. Could she read the guilt behind my love? The fear that every touch, every kiss brought us closer to a truth that might destroy us?

"Then, why do you still feel so far away?" she whispered.

Before I could answer, my phone buzzed with a text message from Kaleb. *Urgent. Call NOW.*

"You should take care of that," Cici said, stepping back. The loss of her touch felt like physical pain.

"It can wait."

She shook her head. "No, it can't. I can see it on your face." Her smile was sad but understanding. "Go. Whatever it is, handle it. I'll be here."

That was the problem. She would be here, waiting, trusting, while I juggled impossible choices and mounting secrets. Loving her had always been the easy part. It was everything else that threatened to tear us apart.

I found an empty spot behind the barn to return Kaleb's call. "What's so urgent?"

"It's about Buck."

"What about him?"

"He's been asking questions about Maverick's accident."

My grip tightened on the phone. "Why?"

"Says something doesn't add up. You know how he gets." Kaleb paused. "Port, he's got contacts in law enforcement. If he keeps pushing, we'll both face criminal charges. I falsified evidence, Porter. I could lose everything."

I closed my eyes, remembering Buck's expression when I couldn't tell him I loved him too. How much more would I lose, trying to protect Maverick's secret?

"I'll handle it," I said, even though I had no idea how. "I'm sorry, Kaleb. I never should've—"

"Wait. Fuck, Port. I agreed to it. I switched the blood samples. I'm sorry too, man. I shouldn't be making you feel like this is all your fault. I could've said no, and I didn't."

After hanging up, I stood in the stillness for a few minutes, listening to Cici's voice carrying from the barn—probably checking on Mesa King. Somewhere in the house, Maverick was likely wrestling with his own demons, carrying the weight of recovered memories and fresh guilt. And out beyond the ranch's fences, someone still wanted to destroy everything the Morris family had built.

I pulled out my sobriety chip, running my thumb over the worn surface. One day at a time, that was what we learned in AA. But which day would be the one when all my careful lies finally caught up with me? And who would be left standing when they did? We sure as hell weren't going to come out of it unscathed.

The sight of Cici in Mesa King's stall took my breath away. The morning sun streaming through the barn window lit the highlights in her hair, making my heart clench. Cici Morris was one of the most honest people I knew and had the kindest heart. If only her life could be as simple as this moment—her doing what she loved instead of spending every day fighting for her family's legacy.

She must have sensed my presence, because she looked up and smiled. "Your call go okay?"

"Roaring Fork stuff." At least there was some semblance of truth in my response. Buck did live there. I nearly groaned out loud at how fucked up my thoughts had become.

More than anything, I wanted to cross the space between us, take her in my arms, and never let go. Instead, I nodded and stepped into the stall, keeping a careful distance as we worked. Every brush of her hand, every shared glance, felt like both a gift and a curse.

"He's getting stronger," she said, stroking Mesa King's neck. "A few more days, and he might be able to get into the ring, get some exercise."

"That's good news."

"Yeah." She turned those knowing eyes on me. "Now, if only everything else was getting better instead of worse."

If only, indeed.

"Porter?" Buck's voice carried from the barn doorway, sending chills up my spine. My brother stood there, in his work clothes, looking like he'd been up for hours. Probably had been. "Got a minute?"

Cici squeezed my arm as she passed. "I need to check on Mav anyway."

I watched her go, then followed Buck outside.

"We need to talk," he said in a thick, low voice.

I thought about the cameras, the surveillance footage. "Not here."

He nodded and motioned to his truck. "Let's take a ride."

I didn't ask where we were going, even when he drove straight past Gunnison. I was beginning to think he was taking me to the Roaring Fork, but when we reached Altamont, he pulled off the main road and parked by the river where we'd learned to fly-fish.

"Here's what I wanna know…"

I turned my head, not wanting to see his face.

"You weren't drunk that night, were you?"

"Leave it alone, Buck."

"Look at me, Porter."

I took a deep breath and turned my head. "Leave it alone," I repeated. This time, my words sounded more like the plea they were.

"Explain it to me."

"If I do, you'll be complicit."

"What about Maverick?"

"He doesn't remember. At least not yet."

Buck scrubbed his face. "I was afraid you were going to say that."

"Who else knows, Buck?"

"If Mav doesn't remember, then nobody outside of you and the sheriff."

I hung my head. "He did it because I begged him. You know what will happen if this gets out—"

"It isn't going to. At least not from me."

I studied him.

"I just wanted to understand, Port. And when the shit hits the fan because of this—and it's going to—I want to be able to help."

I shook my head hard when my eyes filled with tears. "You won't."

"What's that supposed to mean? I just said I would."

"There's something I need to tell you, and after I do, you might not want to be around me long enough to take me back to Parlin."

"I'm listening."

"I knew."

I couldn't look him in the eye, but that he hadn't asked what, said it all.

"How'd you find out?" he finally asked.

"Roscoe told me one drunken fucking night. Dumped it all on me, then made me swear on Mama's life that I'd never tell."

"You were eleven when she died."

I nodded. "And I was eight when he told me you were another man's son."

"Fuck," he said under his breath.

"I'm sorry, but don't think that means I'm asking your forgiveness. I get why you can't give it to me."

"Porter…"

I shook my head again as tears streamed down my cheeks. Instantly, I was that eight-year-old kid again, scared shitless, but instead of my father's wrath, I couldn't bear the idea that this was the end of my relationship with my brother.

I felt his hand on my arm. "Porter."

"God, I'm just so…fucking…sorry."

His fingers squeezed my flesh. "Don't."

I wiped at my tears with my sleeve and looked up at him.

"He did this to you. To us. Not just you and me. All of us. Roscoe Wheaton was a mean, abusive *sonuvabitch* who did everything in his power to make us as miserable as he was. This is not your sin, Port. You were a kid."

"And now, I'm a man. One who could have—should have—had the balls to tell you."

He shook his head like I had. "This is the secret an eight-year-old boy was forced to keep. Not who you are now. You know how I know?"

"Nope."

"I just watched you turn into him. I saw it happen. You turned into that scared kid who did everything he could to stay out of Roscoe's line of sight, as far from him as you could get. The same way we all did." His fingers pressed into my flesh a second time, and my eyes met his again. "I forgive you, Porter. You are one-hundred-percent absolved of this."

"But, I didn't—"

He raised a brow. "What? Tell me?"

I nodded.

"What do you call this? What's happening right now?"

"That's not what I meant, and you know it."

"Wrong." His tone was emphatic. "There was no gun to your head, Port. You told me now because it was the right time to do it. Simple as that. You've made your amends to me, little brother."

I stuck my hand in my pocket and pulled out my sobriety chip, rubbing it with the pad of my thumb.

"I'm really proud of you, Porter."

"Thanks." My voice cracked as tears threatened again.

"Not just for that." He motioned to the chip. "But for what you did for Maverick. I'm still worried that this will eventually blow up in your face, but I promise you, no one will hear about it from me."

"How did you find out? At least if I know what evidence there is, maybe I'll have a better idea of when this bomb is gonna explode."

"There isn't any evidence."

I raised a brow.

"Crazy how things go missing sometimes, isn't it? And when I say missing, I mean every last trace."

"How?"

He chuckled. "Some things you're better off not knowing."

"Decker?"

"Sometimes, people can do something without having to know all the whys."

I nodded, understanding what he was saying and that it meant I could never thank Ashford.

"What you said earlier, about Mav remembering, it's gonna happen, and when it does, I don't know what it will do to him."

"If I were you, I'd be more worried about what it's going to do to Cici."

I rested against the back of the seat. "It's all I think about."

"I have a suggestion for you. Figure out a way to tell her. The sooner, the better."

"That's the problem, Buck. I swore to Mav I wouldn't."

"You've got to. Your only hope of saving her, yourself, and her brother is if you get it out in the open. And by that I mean, between the three of you. No one else." Buck started the engine. "You hungry?"

"Not really," I said, chuckling. "Kind of sick to my stomach, if you wanna know the truth."

"Mama always said there's nothing better for a tummy ache than a slopper."

I laughed out loud. "She never said that."

"Well, she should've, cuz I know for a fact that an open-faced cheeseburger smothered in green chili will kill *whatever* ails you."

18

Cici

I watched Porter climb out of Buck's truck, immediately sensing something had changed. It hadn't been more than a couple of hours since I last saw him, but I didn't remember him looking so bone-deep exhausted before he and his brother left.

"Everything okay?" I asked as he approached the porch, where I waited.

"Yeah. Just handling some things."

I studied his face, noting the red puffiness around his eyes that suggested he'd been crying. Porter Wheaton, who faced down charging bulls without flinching, looked like he'd been through an emotional war. The urge to wrap my arms around him, to somehow ease whatever burden he carried, was almost overwhelming.

"Come inside," I said softly. "You look like you could use some coffee."

He followed me into the kitchen, and I felt his eyes on me as I navigated the space I was getting used to sharing with him. The sun streamed through the windows, and while everything looked the same as it had two hours ago, my gut told me it wasn't.

"Did Buck get what he needed?" I asked, trying to keep my voice casual as I poured coffee for both of us.

"Something like that." Porter's hand trembled slightly as he took the cup I offered. Our fingers brushed, sending electricity through my skin despite my growing unease.

Porter leaned in closer to me. "There's something we should talk about. Upstairs."

My eyes opened wide, and I nodded, following him up the steps and into the bedroom when he took my hand.

He shut the door, and I sat on the bed. "The other day, Stetson mentioned a falling out between your dad and his."

"I knew they had. I mean, Dad talked about it. I wasn't very old when it happened. Maybe two or three. What I remember most is that my dad regretted the loss of the friendship. Look, if Stetson has a problem working here—"

Porter shook his head. "He was afraid it was the other way around. That his being here would make you uncomfortable."

"Why would it?"

"I think he just wanted to make sure you didn't think he or his family held a grudge."

"Of course I don't. Plus, he's here to help, right?" I fell back on the mattress. "I need all of that I can get."

Porter lay beside me and took my hand in his.

"Remember that conversation we had about me taking off and lying on a beach somewhere?"

He chuckled. "Yeah, but I don't think I'd call it a conversation."

"Whatever. Anyway, it's sounding damn good right now. Wanna go with me?"

He brought my hand to his lips and kissed the back of it. "I'd like nothing better, and when the time comes that you're serious, I'll be all in."

I turned to look at him and caught him flinch. "What was that about?"

"What?"

"You don't have to pretend you want to do something you don't. It isn't like you thought I was serious."

When I tried to pull my hand away, he held on tighter. "There's just a lot going on right now."

My mouth gaped. "I wasn't suggesting now. Jesus."

He rolled to his side so he was facing me. "I know you weren't. I just"—he took a deep breath and let it out slowly—"wish we could escape for a while too."

"I couldn't leave Mav."

He nodded. "Neither could I. Listen, this goes against the tenets of the organization, but I've been taking Mav to—"

"Don't tell me. If you aren't supposed to tell me, I don't want to hear it." I turned to face him. "I know that whatever you're doing is helping."

"One day at a time," he said under his breath.

What I was about to say—to suggest—might backfire on me in a spectacularly mortifying way, but I couldn't help myself. "Later, when it's time for bed, I want you to get under the covers with me, Porter."

He studied me. "Cici...I..."

I rolled to my back and looked up at the ceiling. "Forget I said anything."

When Porter shifted off the bed, I expected him to leave. Instead, he stretched his body out on mine. "Am I hurting you?" he asked, propping himself up with one arm.

"I like feeling you on top of me."

"You should never doubt how much I want to be with you."

I wriggled my hips and giggled. "I can tell."

"But there are things you need to know, not all of which I can tell you right now."

My eyes scrunched. "I knew you were keeping things from me." When he shifted a second time, I stopped him. "Stay where you are."

He leaned down and kissed me. "You know this is torture, right?"

"Like it isn't for me?" I put my finger on his lips to stop him from saying more. "Tell me this much. Will whatever it is hurt me?"

This time, when he rolled to the side, I let him. "You will be hurt, Cici, but not because any of it is meant against you. Does that make sense?"

"I'll be hurt that you kept whatever it is from me."

"That's right."

I thought it over for several seconds. "If you *could* tell me, would you?"

"So fast your head would spin."

"That's good enough for now, Porter. Just don't keep it from me forever."

"I promise I won't."

19

Porter

After crawling under the covers like Cici wanted me to, I pulled her into my arms rather than wait for her body to turn to mine like it did every night. Holding her felt right. Doing more than that, didn't.

Today seemed like another of the longest of my life, the same way every day had since I arrived at Morris Ranch. While I'd finally been able to confess the secret I held onto and dreaded revealing about Roscoe not being Buck's father, it seemed like, every time an issue was resolved, something else slid into its place.

There weren't many people I'd admired more than Cici's father, not that it meant I was blind to his faults. Like with most people who'd passed away—with the exception of my father—the majority of those who knew him or his wife, focused on the positive rather than remembering the bad shit. Hank had a temper. One he tried hard to hide from his kids and even his wife. I'd only seen it when he had no idea I was paying attention. I didn't like seeing it then, and I didn't like thinking about it now.

"You're keeping me awake," Cici muttered.

"I am?"

"All that loud thinking." She buried her head in my chest.

"Sorry."

"Anything you want to talk about?" she asked.

"Not really."

"Then, keep it down."

I smiled and pulled her closer, wishing so hard that I could remove her clothes and mine and be skin to skin. Not yet, though. Not until I figure what the hell to do about Mav. Buck was right. I needed to tell her what had really happened that night. Actually, Mav needed to, but until he remembered—if he remembered—how could he?

"Porter." My name sounded more like a growl.

"What? I'm not doing anything."

She raised her head. "Do you really not know how much your body wiggles when you're talking to yourself?"

I chuckled. "It does not."

"Try thinking about something that's bothering you. Do it and see if you can stay still. Right now."

"I can't just think about something that's bothering me on demand, Ceec."

"What about Mav?"

I groaned. "Yeah, well…"

"See? You just wiggled."

"No, I didn't." I laughed out loud when she pinched my side. "I can go sleep somewhere else if you'd like."

She glared at me. "What I'd like is for you to *sleep*, and if you're not going to, then put that wiggle to better use."

"God, I love you."

The smile left her face. "I love you, Porter."

"We'll get through this. I promise."

She rested her head on my chest. "I hope so."

"We will." We had to. Now that I was sober, I couldn't walk away from Cici like I did once before. Then, I believed I was saving her. What I was doing instead was hiding who I really was from her. Hiding how much I relied on booze to get me through each day.

"Porter?"

"Yeah?"

"If you break my heart again, I'll kill you."

I shook my head at how well she read me. If I wasn't keeping so many secrets from her, I'd swear she could hear my thoughts.

When I woke with the sun, Cici was still next to me, but sometime in the night, she'd turned so she wasn't facing me, and I hated it. She never did that. Not in the last few days, and not before. Why had she? Was my body moving too much in my sleep?

Unable to resist, I leaned over and kissed the soft spot between her neck and shoulder. One taste, and I couldn't stop myself from taking more. When I ran my tongue up the taut muscle of her neck, Cici groaned.

"Don't start something you aren't gonna finish, cowboy."

"I don't like it when you sleep with your back to me," I whispered.

Cici took my hand and pulled it until it rested on her breast. "I don't like it when you don't touch me."

"God, Ceec." I nearly came undone when she moved the same hand down between her legs.

"Please, Porter. You know what I want."

I knew exactly what she wanted and how. I slid my fingers down the front of her pajama bottoms and inside her panties, pressing the length of one against her clit, then sliding it down farther so just the tip was inside her.

When she started to move so I'd go deeper, I stilled. "You know what I like too, Cici."

She froze. "Please, Porter," she whined.

I reached down more, and her thighs fell open.

"That's what I like, baby," I murmured as I thrust two fingers into her pussy.

"I can't hold back," she warned me.

"Don't. Go ahead and take what you need."

She ground against my hand, her back arching when her heat clenched my fingers. When she whimpered, I pressed my hardness between the cheeks of her tight bottom, wishing so much I could let go, let myself sink into the place that had always felt like exactly where I belonged.

We both froze when a rap on the bedroom door came seconds after we heard Mav's uneven footfalls on the hallway's wood floors.

"Porter? Are we goin'?"

"Yeah. Give me a sec."

"Be in the kitchen."

Cici and I both listened as he made his way down the stairs.

"Are there any meetings that aren't at the butt crack of dawn?" Cici whined.

I didn't miss her acknowledgment of where her brother and I went most every day. "This is cowboy country, Ceec. We've got chores to get back to."

"Tell me somethin' I don't know." She looked over her shoulder at me. "Speaking of cowboys, don't the guys from the Roaring Fork have to get home? I mean, do we still need them here every day?"

I shifted so I could see her face. "Why? Did something happen?"

"No." She hesitated just enough that I knew something had.

"Talk to me, Cici."

"Has it escaped your attention that I am the only woman on this ranch?"

"Did someone hit on you?" If my hand wasn't still down her pants, I would've clenched my fist.

She rolled her eyes. "No. I'm just not used to having so many people underfoot."

"Like this place hasn't always been overrun by cowboys. What's really going on?"

"I don't like having people here who I don't know. I mean, if it's necessary, that's one thing, but can't my crew and I go back to running the ranch on our own?"

"I think so, but I'd like to talk it over with Steel, Jagger, and maybe Decker. How would you feel about that?"

"Seems reasonable." She removed my hand from between her legs. "Mav's waiting, and I'm going back to sleep."

"If the guys return to the Roaring Fork, your days of sleeping in will come to an end."

"Yeah, yeah. Get goin', Port."

I rolled out of bed, put on a clean set of clothes, and kissed her cheek on my way out.

Mav's eyes barely met mine when I joined him in the kitchen. Was it because of our conversation yesterday, or had he heard his sister's moans of pleasure at my hands?

"Made coffee," he muttered, motioning to the travel mug he must've filled for me.

"Appreciate it." It was the first time he'd done something like that.

"Yesterday, I mentioned remembering something about the accident," he said once we were on the road.

His words felt like a knife in my gut. "Is there more?"

Mav shook his head. "No, but there is something I haven't told anyone."

"Do you want to now?"

"At the meeting."

I nodded, wishing I could set aside my fear that he was about to reveal something in front of a room full of people that could potentially land him, Kaleb, and me in jail. This wasn't about me. If Mav was ready to speak at a meeting, I had to encourage him to do so.

When we arrived, Kaleb was standing near the table where coffee and pastries had been set up. I realized I should've called him to let him know what Buck said about every trace of evidence of what we'd done the night of the accident being gone. Except now, with Mav saying he wanted to talk, the lack of evidence might be a moot point.

"He says he's ready to speak," I said under my breath.

When Kaleb nodded, I could see the same internal struggle I felt. This wasn't about either of us. It was about Mav's journey, and we had to respect that, regardless of the consequences either of us would face.

"The other thing has been taken care of," I said as quietly.

We took our seats but not together. Like always, Mav and I sat in the back.

We were nearing the end of the meeting, and Mav hadn't made a move. Just as I thought he might've changed his mind, he stood.

The guy standing near the front nodded once. The rules were, you could stay where you were and speak, or move to the podium. Mav stayed put.

"I, um, my name is Henry, and I'm an, um, alcoholic."

It was the first time I remembered that he'd been named for his dad but used Maverick instead.

"I get that I'm supposed to talk about my problem with alcohol, so, uh, I guess this is where it all started."

When he pulled a folded piece of paper from his pocket, I remained expressionless. His hands shook as he opened it, and from where I sat, I could see letters cut out of a magazine like the ones Cici had shared. Bile rose in my throat as I read what the note contained before Mav read it out loud.

"Your fault. They were out looking for you," it read.

"So I, uh, got this the day of my parents' memorial service. Someone left it for me at the funeral home. It says it's my fault they died."

The typically quiet room went completely still, as though everyone held their breath.

"The night they died, I was at a party. First time I got drunk. I was fifteen. Every day since, until the last few, I've…done the same thing." Tears ran down his cheeks and dripped onto the paper he held. "I don't know of another way to make the pain stop."

He sat down, hung his head, but handed me the paper. I folded it but didn't give it back. The meeting concluded, but until Maverick got up, I wouldn't. Kaleb walked past us, and I made eye contact with him, but not anyone else. And when Mav did stand once the room was empty, I silently followed him out to my truck, used the fob to unlock it, and drove back to the ranch.

Since he didn't speak, I didn't either. Maybe that was wrong, but I had no idea what to say.

I parked in my usual spot, not far from the ranch house, and cut the engine.

"You think I should tell Cici." He didn't phrase it as a question.

"That's up to you."

"She'll hate me."

I reached over and put my hand on his shoulder. "You know she won't, Maverick. The other thing you know, if you dig really deep, is that what's in this note could very well be someone fucking with you. We don't know why they went out that night. We'll never know."

His tears fell fast, and his body shuddered. "I know."

Disputing his belief wouldn't achieve anything, so I kept my mouth shut other than to say he could trust I would never reveal what he'd said either at the meeting or now. "I do think you should tell Cici, but whether you do or not isn't up to me. It's your decision, and I'll respect it."

Mav used his jacket sleeve to wipe away his tears, then opened the door but hesitated to get out.

His back was to me when he spoke. "Just another one of my secrets you'll keep. Right, Porter?"

20

The morning sun barely warmed the February air as I headed toward the south barn to check on Mesa King. Steam rose from the coffee in my travel mug, a gift from my mom, years ago, that I'd started using again recently. The familiar weight of it in my hand made me miss her with an intensity that caught me off guard.

Porter and Mav had left for town early again, like they did most mornings now. Part of me was glad to see my brother looking steadier, more focused, but I couldn't help but believe something significant had shifted between them. The way they looked at each other, spoke to each other—it was different somehow.

A light frost still coated the grass, crunching under my boots as I walked. Each day, it felt like the ranch, like me, was holding its breath, waiting for the next blow to come. Even Mesa King's usual morning greeting wasn't as enthusiastic, which made me worry that he'd had a setback in his recovery.

I was so lost in thought that I almost missed the conversation coming from behind the barn.

"I could see not wanting to make the kid feel guiltier than he already does, but Cici deserves to know why her parents were out that night," I heard Shaw say.

"It won't change anything," a voice that sounded like Martinez's responded.

My coffee mug slipped from my suddenly numb fingers, splashing hot liquid across my jacket. The scalding heat barely registered through the shock of what I was hearing. The voices carried clearly in the cold morning air as I pressed my back against the barn wall, my heart hammering so hard I was sure they'd hear it.

"If it were your parents, wouldn't you want to know? My God, they died thinking their son was in a fatal accident—" Shaw's voice cracked.

The world seemed to tilt on its axis as their words sank in. My knees buckled, and I had to grip the rough wood of the barn wall to stay upright.

"I can't keep it to myself any longer. There's a very real possibility that what happened that night wasn't an accident. The same way Maverick being drunk wasn't."

"You have no proof…"

I raced away before hearing whatever else Martinez was about to say. I couldn't bear more. My feet carried me toward the house, but Porter's truck wasn't in its usual spot. He and Mav weren't back from town yet.

Once inside, I couldn't breathe, couldn't think. The walls felt like they were closing in on me. I needed air. Needed to move. I took off in the direction of the equipment building, where we stored the ATVs that we typically only used in better weather. Maybe a ride would help clear my head and process what I'd just overheard.

The door creaked when I pushed it open, the sound echoing in the still morning air. Dust motes danced in the weak beam of light from the grimy window. I'd barely taken two steps when something caught my eye—a door to one of the side rooms was slightly ajar. It was one we never used, even when Dad was still alive, except for old tack and equipment we meant to repair but never got around to.

My hand trembled as I pushed the door wider. The hinges creaked, echoing in the empty space. I turned on my phone's flashlight, and its beam revealed signs that someone had been in here.

A battery-operated lantern and a pair of binoculars sat on a makeshift table fashioned from an old crate. Beside it was a rusty metal folding chair.

A familiar scent caught my attention—the same brand of cigarettes Dad smoked before Mom finally convinced him to quit.

My stomach churned as I swept the light around the small space, revealing empty food containers, whiskey, and beer bottles, but not much else besides mouse droppings. There was an underlying stench in the place that I'd say I didn't recall, but who knows when I was last in here? Maybe before I left for college?

Peering through the filthy, stained blind that covered the only window confirmed it looked directly out at our house. That someone had been in this room, spying on Mav and me—now, on Porter and everyone else who'd shown up to help us—made me feel violated in a way I couldn't quite explain.

My flashlight beam caught something wedged behind the crate. When I pulled it free, I saw it was a photo of a man, a woman, and a baby I didn't recognize. I shoved it in my pocket, then backed out of the room, desperate to escape both the physical space and the implications of what I'd found.

There was only one ATV in here, which meant the others must now be stored somewhere else. It was covered in cobwebs, which I brushed away before climbing on, needing to get out in the open air more than ever as today's revelations alone threatened to suffocate me.

The key turned, but nothing happened. I tried again. The engine caught this time, but something felt wrong. The steering was loose. Too loose.

I was about to turn it off when the ATV lurched forward, completely out of my control. The wheel jerked violently in my hands, spinning uselessly as I fought for control. I screamed as it careened toward the wall. Metal screeched against metal as it flipped, pinning my leg underneath. The impact knocked the breath from my lungs, and for a terrifying moment, I couldn't even cry out.

The machine's weight pressed against my leg with devastating pressure. Through the pain, I noticed something odd—a thin wire that shouldn't have been there, trailing from the steering column. Someone had rigged this to fail. The realization that, once again, this wasn't an accident made the panic rise faster in my throat.

Pain shot through my thigh. I screamed for help. The pressure was intense, but I couldn't tell if anything was broken. My mind flashed to Maverick's mangled leg after his accident. Would I end up like him?

"Cici!" Porter's voice carried from outside. Had he and Mav just gotten back? "Where are you?"

"In here!" My voice cracked with panic and relief.

He burst through the door, Steel and Jagger right behind him. Their faces went pale when they saw me trapped beneath the heavy machine.

"Don't move," Porter ordered, already assessing the situation with a calm I'd come to rely on. His eyes met mine, steady and reassuring even as I saw the fear behind them. "We'll get you out."

It took all three of them to lift the ATV enough for me to slide free. Porter's hands ran over my leg. "Call 9-1-1," he shouted while he continued checking for injuries. His touch was gentle but thorough in a way that still managed to send shivers through me despite the situation.

When I tried to get up and my legs trembled, he scooped me into his arms, cradling me against his chest like I weighed nothing.

"The steering's been tampered with," Jagger said in a low voice to Porter.

"Get Kaleb on the phone," he replied through clenched teeth before turning to Steel.

He nodded, pulling out his phone as he followed us to the house.

"I want you to stay inside until the EMTs arrive," Porter said, holding me close as he carried me across the yard. My head rested against his chest, his heartbeat as rapid as my own. "Steel will stay with you."

The words to argue wouldn't come.

"What happened?" Mav gasped, jumping up from where he sat at the kitchen table when Porter carried me inside.

"Accident with an ATV," he said, gently easing me down on the couch. "EMTs are on the way. The two of you need to stay with her while I go back and wait for the sheriff," Porter said, looking between Steel and Mav. Both of them nodded.

As I sat waiting, the words I'd overheard burned in my throat. Should I tell him that our parents died thinking he was hurt or dead? That someone had used him as bait to lure them out that night? The haunted look in his eyes stopped me. He was finally getting better. More stable. I couldn't destroy that progress.

I'd tell Porter first. Let him help me figure out how to handle it. But not yet. Not until I could process it myself.

"You okay?" Mav asked, his voice rough with concern.

I nodded, not trusting myself to speak. I shut my eyes and rested against the couch, trying to quell the nauseating feeling in my stomach. According to Shaw, someone had lured my parents to their death with lies about Maverick. And still, someone was trying to destroy what was left of our family. None of the events were isolated. They couldn't be. The same person who'd put my parents' lives in peril was still here, still working to finish what they started four years ago. And what had he meant when he said it might not have been an accident any more than Maverick being drunk that night was?

Steel took up position near the door, waiting for emergency services to arrive. His presence was both reassuring and somehow oppressive. The wail of unnecessary sirens in the distance made everything feel surreal, like a nightmare I couldn't wake up from.

My leg throbbed where the ATV had pinned it, but the pain felt distant compared to the ache in my chest.

Mom's and Dad's last moments must have been filled with terror for Maverick. They died trying to reach their son, not knowing it was all a lie.

The EMTs said there was no indication my leg was broken, and the pain had already begun to subside.

"You're damn lucky," one of them said as they finished checking my vitals and filling out their report.

The pain pill they gave me started to kick in, making me drowsy, but one thought remained crystal clear—someone had orchestrated all this. My parents' accident, the ranch's decline, the ATV tipping over on me—they were all connected by an invisible thread of destruction.

The same question—why—had me shedding tears of frustration. I pressed my hand to my mouth, fighting back a sob. I couldn't break down. Not now. Not with Mav so close by, Steel standing guard, and Porter out there, trying to figure out who might've tampered with the ATV.

I thought about the photo in my pocket but wouldn't show it to anyone before Porter. Other than my brother, he was the only person I felt certain I could trust. Maybe I was stupid for believing I could, but I couldn't bear the idea that I'd be forced to keep all this inside and handle it alone. I needed him. I just prayed that doing so wouldn't destroy me further.

"Steel?"

"Yeah?"

"Can you tell Porter it looks like someone has been watching us from out there? In one of the side rooms?"

"Will do," he said, typing something on his phone.

The weight of the ranch and all its secrets was becoming too much for me to bear. The place that had been my home all my life began to feel like a trap, and we were all caught in it.

21

Porter

"Hey, Porter?" Jagger called out when I returned to the building where the image of Cici being pinned under an ATV would haunt me for the rest of my life.

"Where are you?"

"In here. On your left," he shouted. "Steel messaged that Cici said she thinks someone has been in here recently."

I pushed the door open wider to walk inside when he pointed to a chair that sat near a window as well as a pair of binoculars.

"Watching the ranch house," I muttered.

"Watching everything," Jagger concurred.

I was about to leave the room and take another look at the ATV when I heard him gasp.

"*Jesus*, look at this," Jagger said, pulling back the corner of an old throw rug.

My phone's flashlight's beam revealed dark stains which had seeped into the concrete floor. "Is that blood?"

Jagger looked up at me. "Sure looks like it."

"Human?"

"Impossible to say for certain without testing the DNA, but yeah, it's likely" Jagger stood and took photos with his phone. "Based on the splatter, I'd say there's a good chance someone or something died in here."

The thought made my skin crawl and turned my stomach. I'd never been much of a hunter, even though it was a big sport in this part of the state.

"We need samples," I said, pulling out my phone to see how far out Kaleb was. "And photos of everything."

"Already on it," Jagger said, holding up evidence bags. Apparently, Decker had made sure his team came prepared for anything.

I sent a message to Buck. *Where are you?* I asked.

RF. What's up?

Something at Morris Ranch you need to see.

Wrapping up a few things here, then I'll head that way.

I glanced up and saw Martinez walk in.

"What's going on?" he asked, looking in the direction of the room where Jagger was.

"Accident with an ATV. This is a crime scene, so I'm gonna need you to step out."

His eyes opened wide. "Was someone hurt? I saw an ambulance headed this way when I was out in the south pasture."

"Cici, but she's okay." He still hadn't moved, so I walked over to him. "Juan, I need you to step outside. The sheriff is on his way now."

"Where's Cici now? Up at the house? Is there anything I can do?"

"Not right now. You can get back to work. If there's anything else we need, I'll let you know."

His eyes scrunched, and I thought he might say something else. Wisely, he walked out instead.

I sent a message to Steel. *Don't let Martinez in the house.*

Roger that, he responded.

No one comes in without my say-so.

Understood.

Something about Martinez's behavior had my hackles up. Rather than wait for Buck to arrive, I called him.

"What do you know about Juan Martinez?"

"Meaning?"

"What's his background?"

"No idea, but I can ask around."

"Yeah, do that."

"You got it, Port. Hey, are you all right?"

I saw Kaleb pull in. "I gotta run. The sheriff just arrived. Just get here as soon as you can."

I ended the call and met Kaleb halfway between where he parked and the equipment building.

"How's Cici?" he asked.

"Steel sent a message, saying the EMTs had checked her out. No apparent injuries. But there's something else you need to see."

He followed me inside, and I pointed to where Jagger was collecting evidence.

"Is that blood?" he asked, stepping into the room.

Jagger looked up. "Yes, sir."

"Looks like someone was using this place to keep an eye on things," Kaleb muttered, taking in the rest of the room, then crouching down to examine the stains more closely. "These are old. Hard to say whether we'll learn anything from them or not. I'll get a forensics team in here to see."

"What are you thinking?" I asked when he looked around the room again and his brow furrowed.

"I remember something about a cold case involving the ranch. Someone in the Morris family was murdered. This may have been where they found the body."

"Seriously? There was a murder on the ranch?"

"It was years ago. Maybe more than twenty. I'll have one of my deputies look into it."

When he stepped out of the room to place the call, I followed.

Someone in the Morris family was murdered? In a place as small as Parlin, I was surprised I hadn't at least heard a rumor about it before now.

Kaleb ended the call. "Wanna fill me in on what happened with the ATV?"

Buck's truck pulled up outside. When he joined us inside, his face was grim. "I talked to a few people—" He stopped short at the scene in the side room. "What the fuck?"

"Did you ever hear anything about a murder on the ranch?" I asked.

Buck shook his head. "Not that I recall."

"According to the files my deputy found, Joshua Deevers was sheriff at the time," said Kaleb. "That would've been twenty years ago. When we're finished here, I'll give him a call and see what he remembers about it."

"Listen, if there's nothing else you need me for, I want to check on Cici."

"Go ahead, Port," said Kaleb. "Forensics will be here soon, and they'll seal everything off. Oh, and can you make sure Martinez, Johnson, and Shaw don't go anywhere before I talk to them? Also, see if Cici can put together a list of who's worked here before Hank and Lillian died until now? I'll want to question people who don't work here anymore too."

"Anything else?" I asked.

"That's all for now. I'll be up to the house as soon as I can."

Buck and I started to walk away, but I heard Kaleb ask me to hold up.

"How's Mav?"

There were two reasons he was asking. First, because Buck had been digging around what happened the night of Mav's accident, and also because of what he'd said in the meeting, earlier.

"Quiet," I responded before turning to Buck.

"I'll give you and Kaleb a minute," my brother said before continuing toward the house.

"We don't have anything to worry about as far as Buck's concerned," I told Kaleb.

He nodded. "That just leaves Mav."

He was right, and his comment about me keeping more than one of his secrets told me the kid might remember more than he was letting on.

"How's Cici doing?" I asked Steel when I came inside and didn't see her or her brother.

"She went upstairs to lie down. Said she didn't have any trouble with the steps."

"And Mav?"

"He went up at the same time."

My eyes met Buck's. "Go ahead," he said. "I want to talk to Steel anyway."

I took the stairs two at a time but knocked on the partially open door when I saw Mav was in the bedroom with her.

"Porter?"

I stuck my head inside. "Sorry to interrupt. I just wanted to see how you were doing."

"I'm okay, but please come in. There's something I need to tell you and Mav at the same time."

My eyes met his, and I wondered if he'd take this opportunity to reveal what he'd said at this morning's meeting to his sister.

"I overheard Shaw and Martinez talking earlier." She turned to Mav and took his hand. "About our parents."

For the second time, his eyes met mine.

My heart stopped. "What did they say?"

"They were arguing about whether they should tell me why they were out that night."

"Cici…" I pulled her close to me with one arm while handing Mav the piece of paper from earlier.

"Tell her," I said to him.

"What?" she asked.

Rather than speak, he unfolded the paper and handed it to her. She looked at it, then at me, then her brother.

"'Your fault. They were out looking for you,'" she read out loud. "Where did you get this?"

"There was an envelope waiting at the funeral home."

Her eyes widened momentarily, then softened. "Oh, Mav," she cried.

I released her, and brother and sister embraced, both sobbing while my mind raced.

Someone had lured Hank and Lillian out that night, using Maverick as bait. Had they slid off the road after the car hit a sheet of ice, or had something far more sinister happened?

22

Cici

My brother's tears soaked through my shirt as we clung to each other. For two years, he'd carried the burden of believing our parents died looking for him. And in that time, he'd drowned his guilt in whiskey while I was too caught up in my own grief to see his pain for what it really was.

A knock at the door made us look up. Buck stood there, his usual confident stance somehow more hesitant. "Kaleb needs to talk to you and Mav downstairs."

"Of course," I said, letting Porter first help me stand, then get down the stairs.

We found Kaleb in the kitchen, his expression grim as he looked up from his notebook. Steel and Jagger stood near the back door, speaking in low tones about security protocols. The domesticity of the scene felt wrong against the weight of what we'd just learned.

"Let's go in the living room, where Cici will be more comfortable," Porter suggested. While I thought about saying I'd be fine at the dining table, my body ached worse with every passing minute.

"Tell me what happened with the ATV," Kaleb said after I settled on the couch, next to Porter, and he, Mav, and Buck sat in chairs.

"Before I do, I need to tell you what I overheard earlier."

Kaleb nodded. "Go ahead."

As I reiterated the conversation between Shaw and Martinez, he took notes.

"I felt…like I couldn't breathe," I said, turning to Porter, who squeezed my hand. "You and Mav weren't back yet."

"Walk me through what happened next," the sheriff prompted.

"I decided to take one of the ATVs out and remembered we stored them in the equipment building. But when I got in there, I only saw one."

He made more notes, and when he raised his head, I continued.

"I noticed a door on the left was open, so I went and looked."

"Tell me everything you noticed."

I described the chair and the binoculars, the empty liquor bottles—everything I could remember. "Oh, and I found this." I reached into my pocket and handed him the photo. "I don't know who they are."

"What happened next?" he asked.

"It freaked me out, so I left the room and went to start the ATV." I told him how the steering felt weird, but before I could cut the engine, the thing just took off and hit the far wall. "I couldn't stop it. It all happened too fast," I explained.

After jotting more notes, he looked up again. "Anything else?"

I shook my head.

"Cici, do you remember ever hearing about a murder that took place on the ranch?" Kaleb asked.

My eyes opened wide. It had been years since I thought about it. "My dad's younger sister. I don't remember much about it, though. I mean, I was a baby when it happened, and neither of my parents liked to talk about it. I do remember him saying it was never solved." I shuddered. "You don't think that has anything to do with what's happening now, do you?"

"I can't speculate on that, but it seems unlikely." Kaleb jotted something else in his notebook, then shut it and looked up at me. "We've cordoned off the building, keeping it as two separate crime scenes, and we'll continue investigating both."

Porter leaned closer to me. "Kaleb knows about the note left for Maverick at the funeral home," he said quietly.

The sheriff cleared his throat. "We'll be looking into that as well. In the meantime, is there anything else you specifically remember happening in the days and weeks leading up to your parents' accident?"

"I was away at school. I came home some weekends, but not all."

"I do," said Maverick.

"What?" I asked.

"Dad was acting strange. Paranoid. He'd go on rides at night and take his gun with him."

"Rides?" Kaleb asked, opening his notebook again.

"Along the fence lines."

"What about your mom? Is there anything specific you recall about changes in her behavior?"

"She…" I paused, thinking back. "She insisted I learn to shoot. Said every woman should know how to handle a gun, but when I think back on it, now, I realize she seemed nervous. Maybe even scared."

"Anything else at all you can think of right now that I should know?" the sheriff reiterated.

"I don't think so."

"There might be something in the other safe," said Mav.

"What other safe?" I asked, looking over at him.

"In the office. Behind the picture of him with Bad Grandma."

"It was his favorite bull," I explained. "I never knew there was a safe behind it. How did you know, Mav?"

"I saw him open it once. Late at night, maybe a week before..." He swallowed hard. "Before everything happened."

"Can we take a look?" Kaleb asked.

"Sure," I said as Porter helped me up, his hand steady at my elbow as we moved to the office. The pain in my leg felt distant compared to the ache in my chest as I lifted the framed photo Mav had said covered the safe.

The locked box was small, embedded in the wall. "Anyone know how to crack this thing?" I asked, only half joking as I looked at the dial, having no idea what the combination might be. I tried my mom's birthday, then mine, then Mav's. Nothing worked.

"I might know," Mav said. I stepped aside and watched. When he got to the third number, the mechanism clicked and the door swung open.

"What was it?" I asked.

Mav pointed to the photo. "The date that was taken."

I looked closer, and sure enough, it was handwritten near the bottom.

"Hang on," said Kaleb when I was about to reach inside. He put on a pair of gloves, and once again, I stepped aside and watched him pull out a small leather book I'd never seen before. I looked over his shoulder when he opened it.

"That's Dad's handwriting."

"Looks like a journal," said Kaleb, turning to the last page that contained writing. "This was dated three days before he died."

I focused on the words my father wrote on the journal's final page that Kaleb held out for me to read. "Can't trust anyone outside the family now. Have to protect them. Have to—" The entry ended abruptly, like he'd been interrupted.

"There's something else," he said, reaching deeper into the safe. He pulled out a letter-size envelope, its seal unbroken. My name was written on the front.

"Let her open it," Porter said.

Kaleb nodded.

Inside was a letter. My vision blurred as I read Dad's words out loud.

Dearest Cici,

If you're reading this, something's happened to me. I've made mistakes—choices that seemed right at the time but have come back to haunt us.

I'm so sorry, little girl. I thought I was pro-tecting you all, but maybe I only made things worse. Whatever happens, know that I love you and your brother more than anything in this world.

Dad

PS. Someday, Porter Wheaton will show up, telling you he made me a promise. Trust him, Cicily Ann. He loves you, heart and soul, just like I love your mama. He just hasn't figured life out yet. He will, though.

I blinked away my tears and rested my head on Porter's shoulder when he put his arm around me.

When I raised my head, I looked for my brother, but didn't see him. "Where's Maverick?" The words had barely left my mouth when Steel's voice cut through the tension.

"Martinez just entered the equipment building through the back entrance," Steel said, his eyes fixed on his laptop screen.

Before any of us could move, Buck leaned in to look at another feed. "Maverick just went in too—through the side door."

"Call for backup," Kaleb ordered, already moving toward the door. His hand rested on his weapon.

Porter was right behind him. "Cici, stay here," he ordered over his shoulder.

"Like hell." I grabbed my father's shotgun from beside the door, checking that it was loaded. The familiar weight of it in my hands brought back memories of my mom insisting I learn to shoot and of the fear I'd sometimes catch in her eyes. Now, I understood why. "You'll have to kill me to keep me from going."

Our eyes met for a fraction of a second, and I saw the moment he accepted there was no arguing with me. "Stay behind me," was all he said.

We moved quickly across the yard, spreading out as we approached the building. The sun cast long shadows, and every movement caught my eye. Something about Martinez being in there made my skin crawl, though I couldn't say exactly why, but something felt very wrong.

Kaleb and Buck circled around to the back while Steel and Jagger approached from where Mav had gone in.

The sheriff motioned for silence as we neared the entrance. The sound of voices carried from inside—Maverick's and another I recognized as Martinez's.

"What are you doing in here?" Maverick's voice was steady despite the situation.

"Finishing what I started." Juan's tone was different—harder, colder than I'd ever heard it. "The fire wasn't enough. The poisoned horse, the sabotaged ATV…none of it was enough."

"What are you talking about?"

"Your father killed mine. Buried him out on the ranch like a dog—"

"You're wrong. My dad never killed anybody," Maverick shouted at him.

Martinez's harsh laugh echoed off the concrete walls. "You think it's hard to kill? It isn't. Your parents, then you, and next, your sister, all of you are getting what you deserve."

"My parents' accident—"

"Accident? No. I made it happen. That call about you being hurt—the one that sent them racing out into that storm?" He paused, savoring the moment. "That was me. So was that note you got at the funeral home. All me, asshole. It was only supposed to be Hank." He shrugged. "But when your mom went along…so be it."

"You're lying," Mav said in a low voice.

"Am I? You sure about that, kid? What about that party where you got so wasted you crashed your truck? Who do you think made sure your drinks were a little extra strong? You think I wasn't there to run you off the road the same way I did them?"

Porter's arm shot out to block my movement forward as my finger tightened on the trigger.

"Why?" Maverick's voice shook. "Why are you doing this to us?"

"An eye for an eye." Metal clinked in the darkness—the sound of a gun being cocked.

Kaleb's signal came sharp and fast as he rounded the corner. *"You're surrounded, Martinez! Drop the gun!"*

The room exploded into chaos. Juan spun, firing blindly. The muzzle flash lit up his face, twisted with hatred. Porter tackled me down as bullets sprayed overhead, shattering wood and glass.

Maverick didn't hesitate. He lunged forward, driving his shoulder into Martinez's midsection like he was taking down a steer. The gun went flying as they crashed to the floor.

He recovered fast, producing a knife from nowhere. The blade slashed through the air where Mav's throat had been seconds before. Porter launched himself into the fray, catching Martinez's wrist mid strike.

They slammed into the wall hard enough that the knife clattered away, but Martinez fought like a rabid animal, landing a vicious headbutt that sent Porter staggering back. Blood streamed from his nose as Martinez dove for his fallen gun.

Maverick, despite his bad leg, swung a length of pipe he'd grabbed in the chaos. It connected with Martinez's ribs with a sickening crack, but he kept coming, fingers inches from the weapon.

Time slowed as I got to my feet, watching him reaching for anything to continue his onslaught of carnage. My father's shotgun felt alive in my hands—familiar weight, smooth wood worn by years of use. Mom's voice echoed in my head: "Wide stance. Lean in. Shoulder locked." I could almost feel her hands adjusting my position like she had so many times before.

My heart thundered, but my hands were steady as I squeezed the trigger. The blast sent a sharp kick against my shoulder, the stock driving back into the pocket where I'd anchored it. Hot powder stung my nose as the sound rolled through the room like thunder. Through the ringing in my ears, I heard wood splinter when the bullet hit the wall and saw Martinez scrambling back. The power of it coursed through my arms, but I held my ground, already shifting to track him if he tried for the weapon again. This was what Mom had prepared me for, though I doubted she'd ever imagined this scenario. The shotgun had always felt too big for me as a kid—now, it felt like an extension of my body, as natural as breathing.

"Freeze!" Kaleb's voice cut through the ringing in my ears, his weapon trained on Martinez's head. "One twitch, and it's over."

Steel and Buck converged from opposite sides as Kaleb moved in with handcuffs. Blood ran down Martinez's face, but his eyes burned with something beyond hatred—pure madness.

"You think this ends here?" he spat as Kaleb secured him. "I've spent years planning this. You'll never stop me."

Porter pulled me close as they led him away, his heart hammering against my back. Maverick leaned against the wall, chest heaving. Every word Martinez had uttered hung in the air between us, too raw to process.

23

Everything was hauntingly still as we made our way from the storage building back to the house. Cici clung to me as we walked across the yard. Buck and Mav were in front of us, and Steel and Jagger followed behind.

Nothing Martinez had said about Hank killing his father made sense, but the other things he'd confessed to did. Hank and Lillian's accident. Even Maverick's. I hadn't seen a third vehicle that night, but now that I thought back on it, the way Mav's vehicle came barreling at me, it seemed likely he'd been forced off the road.

When the shock of what had happened in the last few minutes wore off, Cici would remember what Martinez had said about how drunk Mav was and she'd have questions.

Me? I couldn't help but wonder, now, if fate had put me in his path that night to save his life more than take the fall for his blood alcohol level. If I hadn't pulled him from the vehicle that exploded minutes after I had, he'd be dead—just like Martinez had intended.

Had he stuck around? Witnessed the conspiracy that unfolded that night? I doubted it since if he had, he would've already used it against us. I didn't care about that anymore, though. If I went to jail for what I did, so be it. I prayed Kaleb didn't experience any fallout, but still, I knew I had to tell the truth about what I'd done. Not just that night, but every truth, including that I hadn't shown up at the ranch of my own volition. It hadn't been because of a promise I made Hank. It was because I was forced to be here. I couldn't stomach any more lies, of omission or otherwise.

We'd only been inside for a couple of minutes when Cici asked to be alone with Maverick. As the two siblings made their way up the stairs by themselves, I approached my own brother, needing to both give and get comfort.

"How are you holding up, Port?" he asked.

"Honestly? I could use a drink pretty damn bad." I pulled my chip out of my pocket. "That doesn't mean I'll take one."

"I hear ya," he said, squeezing my shoulder.

I looked out the window and saw Martinez being escorted to the back of the patrol car and Kaleb walking toward the house after he'd shut the vehicle door.

"Fuck of a thing," Buck muttered under this breath.

"Fuck of a thing," I repeated.

"Porter?" I heard Mav say from upstairs at the same time Kaleb came inside.

"Go ahead," he said when I glanced over at him. "We'll talk later."

I took the stairs two at a time, and when I reached the top, found Cici in the middle of the bed, propped up by a pillow. Mav was on the opposite side, where I'd slept the last few nights.

"Come sit with us," Cici said, patting the mattress.

What I wanted to do was stretch out beside her, wrap her in my arms, and beg her to forgive me for everything I was about to tell her. Instead, I sat facing her.

"Porter…"

My eyes met hers, waiting for whatever she'd say, praying it wasn't that she never wanted to see me again.

"I don't remember much about that night," Maverick said, propping himself up on his elbow. "Just bits and pieces."

"I remember everything," I confessed, looking between him and Cici.

"Will you tell us?" she asked, her voice barely above a whisper.

"I met Kaleb, who's not just my friend but also my AA sponsor, for coffee that night…" I reiterated the rest as factually as I could, attempting to keep my voice as free from inflection as possible. When I talked about pulling Mav from his vehicle, Cici's eyes filled with tears, and when I told them both what I'd asked Kaleb to do, she reached for my hand and sobbed. By the time I got to the end, Mav and I were both crying too.

"I hated you," she whispered.

I nodded. "In a lot of ways, I deserved it."

She shook her head. "Never."

I took a deep breath. "There's more I have to tell you. Things that don't concern Maverick."

He brushed his tears and got up. "I'll be in my room if you need me."

"Whatever it is, I don't care," she said once we were alone.

I shook my head. "I have to tell you, Ceec."

"Can you come here at least?" She tried pulling me closer, but I wouldn't budge.

"I wasn't honest about why I showed up here or why I stayed."

Her eyes opened wide. "What do you mean?"

"Your father did ask me to look out for you and Maverick if anything happened to him. That part is true. I'd like to think I would've regardless."

"Regardless of what?"

"Whether I had a choice." I told her about the trust my siblings and I had learned about after my dad died and what Buck had to do in order to keep us all from losing our inheritance. I wasn't supposed to talk to anyone about it, but this was Cici, and there couldn't be secrets between us. Not any longer. "We thought that would be the end of it, but it wasn't. Cord was next." I explained how he'd had to travel to a small town in New York State and that he'd have to remain there for a total of three hundred and sixty-five days.

"Is that why you're here?" she asked. "Because of the trust?"

"It is." When I tried to remove my hand from hers, she held on tighter.

"What if I hadn't let you stay?"

"You did, so honestly, I don't know what I would've done."

"You would've lost the Roaring Fork."

I nodded. "Maybe." I looked down at our clasped hands. "I wasn't honest with you, Cici. That's the bottom line."

She sighed. "You're right. You lied to me, Porter, and I can see why you think I wouldn't forgive you for it."

"I'll understand if you don't."

She raised a brow. "And if I told you to leave, would you?" I opened my mouth to speak, but she shook her head. "Let me finish."

I nodded.

"If, right now, I told you to get out, to leave my property and never come back, would you leave, just like that?"

"No."

"What would you do instead?"

"I'd stay anyway, but not because of the Roaring Fork. I'd stay because I love you, and I'd rather die than ever walk away from you again."

"In the time since you arrived, and even before that, you risked your own life for Mav and me. The night of his accident, in the fire, today when you stopped Martinez from killing my brother. Did you do all that out of guilt?"

"Of course I didn't."

"Don't you think I know that?"

Cici pulled my arm, and this time, I shifted so I could sit beside her and take her in my arms. "What happens at the end of the year?"

"I'm not exactly sure, but for Buck, he was free to do whatever he wanted."

She shook her head. "Not with the trust, with us."

"Nothing. I mean, I don't want to leave, Cici."

"So you'd stay?"

"Yes."

She tightened her arm around my waist. "You wouldn't leave?"

"I would not."

"And you love me?"

I put my finger on her chin and raised it so I could look at her. "I love you, and I'm never leaving you or this ranch."

Her eyes scrunched. "Hmm."

"What? Do you think I'm lying?"

"No, but…"

I studied her. "Whatever it is, just say it."

"My daddy said you love me, heart and soul, just like he loved my mama. He also said you haven't figured out life yet. So, I guess I'll just have to wait."

"Jesus, Porter, even a dumb kid like me can figure out what she's hinting at," Maverick said from right outside the bedroom door.

"Mav! Go to your room!" Cici hollered at him.

"What? I'm trying to help here, Ceec."

"Go away, Mav," she hollered.

We heard him shuffling down the hallway.

"I love you, Cicily Morris, and I'm committed to you, this ranch, and to our future."

"I believe you, Porter Wheaton. And I believe *in* you."

Kaleb returned the following morning, saying he and his interrogation team had gone through a grueling hours-long interview with Juan Martinez. While the story he'd told filled in some of the blanks, there were still so many unanswered questions.

Martinez grew up believing his father had abandoned him and his mother, which, in part, had happened. She'd gotten pregnant when still in high school. The two never married, and she raised Juan in Montrose, where her family resided.

When he turned eighteen, which was six years ago, he visited Parlin, where his mom had once lived, to search for his father or his father's family, who he knew little about. Another point of information—the name on his birth certificate was Juan Garcia.

According to what he'd said in the interrogation, the only living relative he found in Parlin was his paternal grandmother, who said she hadn't seen or heard from her son in over twenty years.

He'd done a lot of asking around, and most people either never knew his dad or didn't remember much about him.

Coincidentally, or so he said, he'd run out of money and was looking for a job when he heard Morris Ranch was hiring hands. Wade Carson was the ranch manager at the time and offered him a minimum-wage job. Wade died shortly after that, and Jack Shaw took over his position. When asked what name he was hired under, he responded he'd used the surname Martinez.

So far, it wasn't clear whether he'd legally changed his name, or if he hadn't, how he was able to collect a paycheck.

A few months into his job, Juan met an old cowboy who said he remembered Esteban Martinez and that he'd also worked for Hank Morris. He'd done some digging and had even asked Shaw and Johnson about him, but neither recalled much about him.

When he ran into Hank Morris one day when they were out moving cattle, he asked him too. While Hank also said he didn't recall anyone by that name, explaining how many ranch hands had worked at Morris through the years, Juan said there was something about his initial reaction that made him suspicious.

It wasn't until almost two years later, when Juan was asked to move a piece of equipment to the storage building, that he stumbled on a photograph, similar to the one Cici found, of a woman he recognized as being his mother. In it, she was holding an infant, and a man Juan suspected was his father, stood next to her.

He'd asked around again, showing people the photo. A local resident told him two things that had changed the course of his life and those of Hank, Lillian, Cici, and Maverick.

According to that man, the rumor at the time was that Hank had killed Esteban, but his body was never found.

When Kaleb asked if anyone had reason to believe Hank killed Esteban, Juan reiterated that no one knew the details, only what they'd heard.

After others repeated the same rumors, Juan was convinced they were true and that Hank was responsible for his father's death.

That marked the beginning of the inexplicable accidents that befell the Morris family.

The details he'd given about certain occurrences were close enough for Kaleb to believe Juan was responsible for the majority, if not all, of the sabotage inflicted on the ranch, animals, and equipment.

"What did he say about the night Hank and Lillian died?" I'd asked.

"He confirmed what we overheard him say to Maverick, saying he'd been the one who called Hank, claiming to be with the sheriff's office and saying Mav had been in a fatal car accident," Kaleb responded.

"It makes sense that my mother would've gone with my dad that night, searching for their son," said Cici, tears running down her cheeks.

Kaleb went on to say that, while there was no evidence to confirm it, Juan's statement about running them off the road that night was plausible.

I knew the sheriff well enough to say that whatever he was about to tell us wasn't going to be easy. His eyes were hooded, and his shoulders drooped in a way most others might not pick up on.

He leaned forward in the chair where he sat and rested his arms on his knees. "Cici, I know we touched on this briefly, but how much did you know about your father's sister's murder?"

"Very little. Like I said, neither of my parents liked to talk about it."

"You asked me if I thought it had anything to do with what was happening now, and I told you I didn't believe so."

She nodded. "I remember."

"I no longer feel that way."

24

Cici

If only I could cover my ears with my hands or tell Kaleb I didn't want to hear whatever he was about to say, I would.

"While there is no evidence that your father killed Esteban Martinez, we did locate his body buried on Morris Ranch property. It's been transported to the county morgue."

"What happens now?" I asked.

"An autopsy will be performed to determine the cause of death. Additionally, we'll use DNA samples to confirm whether it's a match to those collected from your aunt."

"Her name was Constance. She was only twenty when she died. There was a bigger age gap between her and my dad than there is between Mav and me. One thing I did know is she lived here, on the ranch, with my parents after my grandparents both died within a few months of each other. She went to Western State like me." I looked up when I realized I was rambling, but it had become important to me that we talked about her as a person, not as just my father's sister who was murdered.

"I'm sorry, Ceec," said Porter, squeezing my hand.

"I was a baby when it happened," I added, looking into his eyes.

"I know."

I looked up at Kaleb. "You said a match to the DNA collected from my aunt."

He nodded.

"Had she been…?" I couldn't bring myself to say the word, but when Kaleb nodded a second time, I took it to mean he understood what I was asking. "No wonder he killed him," I said under my breath but uncaring whether anyone had heard me. "Does Juan know?"

"If you mean our suspicions, yes."

"Did he before?"

Porter moved so his arm was around my shoulders.

"He said he did not."

"Do you believe Juan's father killed Constance?"

"I do."

"He killed both my parents and tried to kill my brother and me, along with at least one of our horses. He threatened the welfare of an entire herd of cattle and caused thousands of dollars worth of damage." The longer I talked, the louder my voice got. Finally, I stood, clenching my fists. "He burned down my fucking barn!" I shouted. "I should've killed him. I *should've*."

Both my brother and Porter stood, then Kaleb did too.

"I understand why you feel that way," he said.

"Do you?" I shouted at him. "Why did he do all this? Revenge? An eye for an eye? He said those exact words. Well, what about my aunt?" I shook my head hard. "How dare he seek revenge when his father raped and killed her?"

I couldn't stand being in the room another second and stormed out of the house, coming face-to-face with Jack Shaw.

"Cici—"

Before he could say another word, I planted my fist in his face as hard as I could. "You *knew*, you bastard. You knew he lured my parents out there that night. How *could* you? *Get the hell off my land!*"

He turned to walk away, then stopped but didn't face me. "I didn't know about the phone call until recently."

"How recently?"

"Martinez let it slip that a call had come in that night about Mav being in an accident. That was the first I'd heard of it. I questioned him about it, and he said that was all he knew, that he couldn't remember who'd told him. Then he added he thought it might've been Johnson, but when I asked him, he said that, like me, he'd never heard about a phone call."

"You should've told me right away," I shouted at him. "You should've—" I dissolved in tears and would've fallen to the ground had Shaw not caught me.

"I'm sorry, Cici. If I could go back and do it over, I would."

"Jack, the sheriff wants to talk to you and Johnson," said Porter, taking me in his arms when Shaw let go.

I clung to him as sobs racked my body. "He avenged the death of a rapist and murderer," I cried.

"He did." Porter stroked my hair, holding me until I could finally catch my breath.

"Thank you for not defending him," I said, wiping my face with my shirtsleeve.

His eyes scrunched. "I never would. Whether he knew what his father had done or not is no justification."

"My dad killed him."

He nodded. "That's very likely true. I'm not sure it will be proven, but…"

"I know he did. I'm sure Maverick does too." I pointed to my chest. "In here."

"I'm sure he felt justified," Porter whispered, but I shook my head.

"Earlier, when I said I should've killed him when I had the chance, I know that if I had, it would've been something I never would've gotten over. Taking a life. I doubt my dad did, either." I thought about his letter and how he'd said he made mistakes. I didn't doubt Martinez's death was what he was referring to.

I was facing the house and saw the sheriff step out onto the porch and shield his eyes from the sun.

When Porter noticed too, we walked toward him together.

"I wanted you to know as soon as I heard. The DNA was a match. There were also signs of trauma on Constance's body that were consistent with someone of Esteban Martinez's size. His hands in particular."

"He strangled her?" I asked.

"Yes, and that was the cause of death."

"How did he die?"

"Gunshot wound. According to the medical examiner, he was shot in the back."

"Is there anything that proves my dad…?"

"No, Cici, unless there was a witness who hasn't come forward."

I looked beyond him to where Shaw and Johnson stood. "I wonder how much they really know."

Kaleb nodded. "They've agreed to come to the office and give their statements. If I learn anything new, I'll let you know right away."

I thanked him, then said I wanted to check on Maverick. Porter stayed behind to talk to him, but said he'd be right behind me.

"Hey," I said when my brother met me inside the door. "How are you doing with all this?"

He hung his head. "Honestly? I want a drink. More like a whole bottle."

I nodded, keeping my eyes riveted to his, but unsure what to say.

"I'm gonna ask Porter if there's a meeting."

My eyes filled with tears, but I smiled. "I think that's a very good idea."

My little brother, who towered over me, pulled me into his arms. "I'm so sorry for all this, Ceec."

"Me too."

The door opened, and Porter stepped inside, closing it behind him. "Kaleb's heading back to the office now. He said to give him a call if you needed anything."

He was looking at me, so I motioned to my brother. "I think there's something Mav wants to talk to you about."

I went into the kitchen and picked up my dad's coffee mug that had sat in the spot by the maker since the night he died. I washed and dried it, then put it in the cupboard where we kept the others, sliding it to the back. I wasn't ready to get rid of it, and maybe I'd never be, but I didn't feel bad putting it away now. Just like wiping away the coffee ring that was beneath it didn't feel wrong.

"We're gonna head into town," said Porter. "Do you want to ride along?"

"I think I'll stay here, maybe clean the house."

"Ceec, I can do that," Mav offered.

"I want to." The truth was, I wanted to walk from room to room, remembering my parents without feeling as though I needed to look out the window or worry what horrible thing might happen next.

"If you go out—"

"I'll let Steel or Jagger know," I assured Porter.

"We won't be long."

I nodded and kissed his cheek, then my brother's, before going upstairs. I lay on the bed for a few minutes, which was where Porter found me over an hour later. I'd fallen asleep, and it had been peaceful.

When I opened my eyes and saw him beside me, I rolled closer. "I didn't clean the house," I confessed.

"There will be plenty of time for that later or tomorrow or the day after that."

"I'm sorry you can't go home, Porter."

"Home? Isn't that where I am?"

"It's Morris Ranch, not the Roaring Fork."

He shrugged. "I've been thinking that, rather than let them hang onto a roughstock program I developed, I should move it here. Once the north barn is rebuilt, that is."

"Err, okay. I mean, can you do that?"

He shrugged. "Cord can't leave New York until December, so he isn't gonna care. I doubt Bridger or anyone else will miss the extra work."

"I'm not sure what to say. I mean, if you're asking me if it's okay, it is."

"I'm thinking we could partner, ya know?"

"Morris-Wheaton Roughstock Contracting?" I teased.

"You know what would sound better? Morris-Wheaton-Wheaton."

My eyes scrunched, and we both laughed.

"Yeah, that sounds terrible. I'm sure we'll be able to come up with something better after, you know, we're married. That's if you'll marry me, Cici."

I looked down at the ring I hadn't noticed him take out of his pocket.

"Porter? Are you seriously…?"

"Proposing?"

I nodded.

"Should I get down on one knee? Am I doing it wrong?"

I held out my hand. "You won't be once you slip that diamond ring on my finger."

"I think you're supposed to say yes first."

"Yes!" I shouted, throwing my arms around him. "Yes, yes, yes!"

"Woohoo!" I heard my brother yell from right outside the bedroom door.

"Okay if he comes in?" Porter asked.

"Yes, but I need to ask you something first."

The smile left his face, but his eyes remained riveted to mine. "Go ahead."

"When you said Morris-Wheaton-Wheaton, did you mean Maverick would be the Morris?"

"I did. It's his legacy too."

"Do you think he'll, you know, want to be a part of it?"

Porter smiled. "It was the only way he'd give me permission to marry you."

25

We'd worked hard in the months since we put Martinez's arrest and subsequent conviction behind us.

Morris Ranch entered into a formal partnership agreement with the Roaring Fork as well as the Flying R, Matt Rice's outfit. Together, the three ranches formed the largest roughstock contracting business in the state of Colorado. Third largest in the country.

The hands from the Roaring Fork who'd helped with the bull program there worked at Morris instead, led by Bullet Simmons, who was now the assistant bull manager at our facility, under Maverick.

Roaring Fork's equine program remained over in Crested Butte, where Stetson Hamilton was able to put much of what he'd learned from his father into practice. While the Flying R raised some bucking bulls and broncs, the majority of what they were responsible for were animals for the timed events—things like team roping and bulldogging.

The new company was making our formal debut at this month's National Western Stock Show, the biggest event of its kind in the world, which had been around since 1906. Since it went on for two weeks and I was still bound by the trust to not be away from Morris Ranch for longer than forty-eight consecutive hours, I'd be doing a lot of traveling back and forth on the four-hour route between Denver—the home of the NWSS—and Parlin. That meant I was the main transport guy when animals needed to return to their respective ranches or when others were ready to be delivered.

Cici rode with me, and part of what we did on the way was plan our wedding. Actually, the wedding part had been handled quickly when every idea Cici came up with was met with agreement from me. It was the honeymoon that took the longest and where we had the most fun, talking and dreaming about the places we wanted to visit.

That I couldn't leave until the end of February was the reason we'd delayed it and the "official" ceremony. Cici and I became husband and wife in July, with Maverick and the justice of the peace's spouse as our only witnesses. The only people who knew, outside of us, were those who'd signed the roughstock business agreement since, on it, her name read Cicily Morris-Wheaton.

"I still can't believe I met Robert Short in person or that we have straws of Brazen's semen in that cooler on the backseat," said Cici on our ride home.

Robert Short had been considered "rodeo royalty" since I was a kid. He'd also revolutionized professional bull riding by being the first to offer the straws of semen we'd purchased versus paying actual stud fees.

The partners had collectively agreed to make the investment to breed using sperm from the animal once known as the "most dangerous bull in the world." While no riders had died after being bucked off Brazen, several had been injured. In his career, only two riders had managed to stay on him for the required eight seconds, and that was only one of the things that made the bull famous. And while we had no desire for any of his progeny to be considered *dangerous*, we knew our investment would pay off many times over just based on the DNA of the animals sired.

"Snickers," she said under her breath, chuckling. "I still can't believe my brother named a prized stallion after a candy bar."

I laughed too. "The story he told is true, Ceec. It was the candy bar that was originally named after a racehorse that belonged to the Mars family."

She looked over at me with wide eyes. "I thought he made that up."

I smiled and shook my head. "All true."

She rested her head against the seat, and the smile left her face. "A year ago, my brother almost died."

I nodded. It had been exactly one year since I pulled Maverick from a vehicle that exploded minutes later. I had no idea what the man or woman executing the Roaring Fork Trust had in mind when they sent me to Parlin in order to fulfill the terms of a codicil, but like Buck and Cord before me, that they had, changed my life for the better. I may never have reconnected with the woman I loved, heart and soul, just like Hank had said in his letter.

I wondered who would be chosen next to spend three hundred and sixty-five days of their life somewhere they couldn't leave for more than forty-eight hours. I had two siblings left—Holt and Flynn—and if either received that news, I had no idea how they'd make it work.

Holt was in an internationally famous rock band with Matt Rice's brother. They spent most of every year out on the road, on tour. My only sister and the baby of the family, Flynn, was married, and she and her husband had one-year-old twin boys.

Then again, maybe I'd be the last required to spend a year of my life somewhere in order for my siblings and me to hold on to our family's legacy.

"What are you thinking about?" Cici asked.

"The Roaring Fork Trust."

She reached over and rested her hand on mine. I brought it to my lips.

"If anyone had told me a year ago that this was what my life would look like, I never would've believed them."

"Same," she said, giggling. "I hated you. Or so I thought. What they say about there being a fine line between it and love is so true. Now, I don't know how I ever thought I could live my life without being married to you." She sighed and looked out the window. "I just hope Maverick finds a love like ours someday."

"He may already have," I blurted.

"With who?" Cici gasped.

"That's Maverick's story to tell."

Keep reading for a sneak peek at

the next book in Heather Slade's

Roaring Fork Ranch series,

Roaring Fork Rockstar

He's a rock star bound by family legacy.
She's a single mom fighting for her daughter's life.
Together they discover love can heal
the deepest wounds.

HOLT

I had it all—world tours with CB Rice, my songs on the radio, everything I ever dreamed of. Except now, it's my turn to fulfill the requirements of a family trust I'd foolishly hoped wouldn't involve me. If I don't spend three hundred and sixty-five days straight in my hometown of Crested Butte, Colorado, my siblings and I will lose our inheritance along with our family legacy. What else is the secret trustee forcing me to do? Play gigs in a local bar and donate my earnings to a kids' charity. It's not the money I'm worried about; I'm making plenty of that from royalties. Instead, it's watching my shot at stardom slip away. The only bright spot of playing night after night at the Goat is its owner, Keltie Marqucz, who serves up mysteries I can't resist. Like why the rattling cough of her tiny daughter, whose wild dark curls frame her face like her mama's do, haunts my dreams.

KELTIE

The last thing I need is Holt Wheaton asking questions about my daughter. He's supposed to be on tour with CB Rice, not playing at my bar, not looking at my little girl like she holds answers to questions he doesn't even know to ask. Every time he picks up that guitar, I see pieces of a puzzle that could shatter everything. His family's past and my daughter's future are tangled in ways that could break both our hearts—or maybe heal them. If only I could tell him the truth.

1

Holt

The strings of my Gibson hummed under my fingers, a familiar comfort in the chaos of the last twenty-four hours. From my perch on the worn stage of the Goat, I could almost pretend this was just another Thursday night in Crested Butte. Almost.

But the envelope in my back pocket said otherwise. The one with CB Rice's official logo and tour sched-ule—forty-eight cities, eighteen countries. The kind of tour I'd dreamed about all my life. The kind that makes songwriters legends. The kind I couldn't be a part of.

My phone buzzed again—probably Remi, CB Rice's manager, asking for the hundredth time if I'd lost my mind. How could I explain that sometimes the biggest dreams come with invisible strings? That sometimes the past reaches out and snags you just when the future seems brightest?

The trust was clear: stay in Crested Butte for three hundred and sixty-five days, or my siblings and I would lose everything. Simple math, impossible choice. My share of the tour earnings would have given me the means to launch my own. Record my own music. Now, I had to watch my dream slip away while donating half my local gig money to a children's charity I'd never heard of.

"Your usual, Holt?" Keltie Marquez's voice cut through my thoughts. She stood at the edge of the stage, a glass of whiskey in her hand, looking at me like she could see right through my carefully constructed calm. That was the problem with small towns—everyone thought they knew your story.

But they didn't know about the trust. About the way my father's voice still echoed in my head: "Music won't feed cattle, boy."

The stage lights dimmed, casting shadows across the bar's worn floorboards. From here, I could see the old photograph of the Goat's original opening day. Something about it nagged at me like a wrong note in a familiar song.

"What's up?" Keltie asked after sliding the whiskey closer, which I downed in one gulp.

"Nothin'," I replied, running my fingers across the guitar strings once more. The emerging melody was unfamiliar, something sad and sweet and ancient, like a lullaby half-remembered from childhood.

Keltie stilled, her eyes widening just slightly. "Where did you learn that song?"

"I didn't," I said, but my fingers kept playing, muscle memory I shouldn't have. "It's just…there." Like a secret someone had whispered almost too quietly for me to hear.

There was something I was missing with the trust—obvious like a word on the tip of my tongue that I couldn't pull out of my head. All I knew was that whatever it was would shake me, my brothers, and sister to our collective core. I couldn't explain the premonitions that had started coming to me when I was a kid. The first was that my mama was going to die. To this day, I hadn't told anyone that, at seven years old, I knew our mother had cancer before she or our father breathed a word of it.

I looked up at Keltie, who, like me, appeared lost in thought, but before I could thank her for a drink or order another one, a feeling of dread so powerful it made me sick to my stomach came over me,. "I need a minute," I said, setting my guitar on its stand and racing out of the bar's back door.

"Hello. Who are you?" said a little girl I'd almost knocked down when I barreled outside.

"I'm Holt Wheaton," I said. "Who are you?"

"I'm Luna. My mommy owns this bar." I should've known she was related to Keltie. Just like her mama, the girl's dark curls were wild around her face and her brown doe eyes bored into mine like she could read my every thought.

"*Vete para adentro ahora, pequeñina,*" said the older woman with her, who I didn't recognize. Since I spoke Spanish fairly well, I knew she'd said something like, "Go inside now, little one."

"It was nice to meet you, Mr. Wheaton," Luna said, holding out her hand for me to shake. It felt tiny and fragile when I grasped it. But worse, the feeling I'd had that sent me outside in the first place intensified. Something was wrong with her, something bad. I was as certain of it as I was of my own name.

About the Author

USA Today best-selling author Heather Slade writes shamelessly sexy, edge-of-your seat romantic suspense.

She gave herself the gift of writing a book for her own birthday one year. Sixty-plus books later (and counting), she's having the time of her life.

The women Slade writes are self-confident, strong, with wills of their own, and hearts as big as the Colorado sky. The men are sublimely sexy, seductive alphas who rise to the challenge of capturing the sweet soul of a woman whose heart they'll hold in the palm of their hand forever. Add in a couple of neck-snapping twists and turns, a page-turning mystery, and a swoon-worthy HEA, and you'll be holding one of her books in your hands.

She loves to hear from her readers. You can contact her at heather@heatherslade.com

To keep up with her latest news and releases, please visit her website at www.heatherslade.com to sign up for her newsletter.

MORE FROM AUTHOR HEATHER SLADE

ROMANTIC SUSPENSE

K19 SECURITY SOLUTIONS TEAM ONE
Razor's Edge
Gunner's Redemption
Mistletoe's Magic
Mantis' Desire
Dutch's Salvation

K19 SECURITY SOLUTIONS TEAM TWO
Striker's Choice
Monk's Fire
Halo's Oath
Tackle's Honor
Onyx's Awakening

K19 SHADOW OPERATIONS TEAM ONE
Code Name: Ranger
Code Name: Diesel
Code Name: Wasp
Code Name: Cowboy
Code Name: Mayhem

K19 ALLIED INTELLIGENCE TEAM ONE
Code Name: Ares
Code Name: Cayman
Code Name: Poseidon
Code Name: Zeppelin
Code Name: Magnet

K19 ALLIED INTELLIGENCE TEAM TWO
Code Name: Puck
Code Name: Michelangelo
Code Name: Typhon
Code Name: Hornet
Code Name: Reaper

K19 GENESIS CONSORTIUM TEAM ONE
Blackjack's Ascent
Dagger's Shield
Sundance's Trail
Nomad's Compass
Preacher's Decree

K19 SENTINEL CYBER TEAM ONE
Code Name: Admiral
Code Name: Dante
Code Name: Grit
Code Name: Tank
Code Name: Atticus

K19 SENTINEL CYBER TEAM TWO
Code Name: Kodiak
Code Name: Paragon
Code Name: Vex
Code Name: Shredder
Code Name: Jagger

PROTECTORS UNDERCOVER TEAM ONE
Undercover Agent
Undercover Emissary
Undercover Savior
Undercover Infidel
Undercover Shadow

ROYAL AGENTS OF MI6
Make Me Shiver
Drive Me Wilder
Feel My Pinch
Chase My Shadow
Find My Angel

THE INVINCIBLES TEAM ONE
Code Name: Deck
Code Name: Edge
Code Name: Grinder
Code Name: Rile
Code Name: Smoke

THE INVINCIBLES TEAM TWO
Code Name: Buck
Code Name: Irish
Code Name: Saint
Code Name: Hammer
Code Name: Rip

THE UNSTOPPABLES TEAM ONE
Code Name: Fury
Code Name: Merried

MORE FROM AUTHOR HEATHER SLADE

<table>
<tr><td>

WINE COUNTRY ROMANCE

BUTLER RANCH
Kade's Worth
Brodie's Promise
Maddox's Truce
Naughton's Secret
Mercer's Vow
Kade's Return
Butler Ranch Christmas

WICKED WINEMAKERS
CENTRAL COAST
FIRST LABEL
Brix's Bid
Ridge's Release
Press' Passion
Zin's Sins
Tryst's Temptation

WICKED WINEMAKERS
CENTRAL COAST
SECOND LABEL
Beau's Beloved
Cru's Crush
Bit's Bliss
Snapper's Seduction
Kick's Kiss

WICKED WINEMAKERS
RUSSIAN RIVER VALLEY
FIRST LABEL
Bas' Blend
Hux's Harvest
Wolf's Want
Oak's Vintage
Cooper's Claim

</td><td>

COWBOY ROMANCE

COWBOYS OF
CRESTED BUTTE
A Cowboy Falls
A Cowboy's Dance
A Cowboy's Kiss
A Cowboy Stays
A Cowboy Wins

ROARING FORK RANCH
Roaring Fork Wrangler
Roaring Fork Roughstock
Roaring Fork Rockstar
Roaring Fork Rooker
Roaring Fork Bridger

SANGRE VISTA RANCH
Thorn's Stand
Stetson's Storm
Maverick's Reckoning
Cinch's Wager
Flints Chance

</td></tr>
</table>

HEATHER SLADE WRITING AS
MERRIGAN CALDER

DARK ROMANCE

THORNED THISTLE

Commanded

Possessed

Obsessed

Captured

Surrendered

NEW SERIES COMING SOON

CRIMSON CHALICE

VELVET VIPER

www.ingramcontent.com/pod-product-compliance
Lightning Source LLC
Chambersburg PA
CBHW071404300726

48976CB00006B/1979